My Brilliant Life and other Disasters

CATHERINE WILKINS

nosy crow

First published in the UK in 2013 by Nosy Crow Ltd
The Crow's Nest, 10a Lant Street
London, SE1 1QR, UK

Nosy Crow and associated logos are trademarks and/or registered
trademarks of Nosy Crow Ltd

Text © Catherine Wilkins, 2013
Cover illustration © Sarah Horne, 2013
Interior illustrations © Sarah Horne, 2013

3 5 7 9 10 8 6 4 2

A CIP catalogue record for this book is available from the British Library

Printed and bound in the UK by Clays Ltd, St Ives Plc
Typeset by Tiger Media Ltd, Bishops Stortford, Hertfordshire

Papers used by Nosy Crow are made from wood grown in
sustainable forests.

ISBN: 978 0 85763 159 6

www.nosycrow.com

For Pat, Christopher, Joy and Colin.

C. W.

Chapter 1

"Jess, are you even listening?" asks Natalie.

"Yes, of course I am," I lie. But actually I was miles away, thinking about the comic.

"*So...?*" says Nat. I'm grudgingly transported back to our desks in 6C. I try and turn my blank look into a thoughtful face.

It's nearly the end of lunch on Tuesday. Natalie and Amelia are planning what to do at Amelia's sleepover on Saturday. But the thing is, I'm absorbed in *much* more important matters: I've had a brilliant idea for a cartoon about a bee and a wasp having an argument.

"Well?" Nat prompts. "Which sweets should we get?"

"Oh, um. Well, I like fizzy wands," I reply.

"Yes, but not everybody likes the fizzy ones," says Amelia.

Honestly, was it really worth interrupting my train of thought for *this*? Sometimes I just don't think Natalie and Amelia appreciate that I am part of a *Global Creative Enterprise* now. (I mean, you know, potentially – in the future – you have to aim high.) Tomorrow is the big unveiling of the comic fanzine that I've been working on with Joshua and the others. I'm *very* excited about it.

"Well, how about a mixture of both fizzy and non-fizzy sweets?" I suggest patiently.

Don't get me wrong; I am super glad that Nat and I made up. Natalie has been my best friend since we first heard tell that Old McDonald was the sole proprietor of a bizarrely musical farm. And it was just *awful* when we weren't speaking last term.

"Yes, but *which ones*?" asks Amelia.

But at the same time, I can't help but feel this is too much effort to put into planning a sleepover. Surely sleepovers are just meant to be *fun*? Sometimes it seems like all they do is admin.

In fact, now I can't quite believe I was so jealous when Natalie went off with snooty new girl, Amelia. Especially as, since being allowed into their special secret world, I've found out the main activity seems to be list-making.

"I don't know, which ones are there?" I ask.

"I'll make a list," says Nat. (*See?*) She gets out a pen and paper. Amelia starts dictating, and I feel myself starting to zone out again.

"We should definitely get some liquorice, as my cousin Scarlett loves it," Amelia is saying. "I can't wait for you to meet her, babes. She's just *amazing*."

Babes. I frown. And not Scarlett *again*. Amelia is so ecstatic that her "super-amazing, super-cool" cousin can make it on Saturday, that's practically all she can talk about.

If Amelia is to SUPER-AMAZING be believed, Scarlett has single-handedly invented fashion, music and the Internet. And my general rule of thumb is: if Amelia thinks something is amazing, I probably won't.

Still, the main thing is, we're all getting on *really well* now.

"You don't have to come, you know," Amelia says

to me then, clocking my expression.

Well, we're *very nearly* getting on *really well*. It's almost going swimmingly. You know, in the bits where it's not going terribly.

"Why are you saying that?" I ask.

"Well, why are you pulling that face?" asks Amelia.

"What face?"

"Like, you're above this and I'm boring you," says Amelia.

"That's just my face!" I protest. "Though, in truth, I *do* think I'm above this, and you *are* boring me," I add, just not out loud. But how did Amelia pick all that up from a frown?

There's nothing like a good ceasefire. And this is *nothing* like a good ceasefire. Ha ha. I've still got it. *Hmmm.*

Amelia and I are like chalk and cheese. Or, like chalk and a really mean, snooty bully, who joins the chalk's school at the start of Year Six and takes the chalk's best friend away; and goes on about how unfashionable and immature the chalk is; and forms a secret gang

4

and doesn't let the chalk join it, forcing the chalk to respond by forming a rival secret gang. (I am the chalk in this scenario.)

Though to be fair to Amelia, since we all made up she has pretty much knocked most of that on the head, and she's stopped referring to my clothes as "Primarni" altogether.

In fact, in a bid to end the turmoil and bury the hatchet represented by our opposing secret gangs (that were never very secret), Amelia united us the only way she knew how: with admin.

Instead of just disbanding our rival gangs, Amelia thought it would be better to *merge* them under a new umbrella gang name. It had to be a new name, she said, as otherwise "we'd just want to use our own gang's name".

She wasn't wrong about that – my gang had a *brilliant* name. It was called "Awesome Cool Enterprises", or ACE for short (thank you, thank you very much). Amelia and **AWESOME COOL ENTERPRISES** Natalie's gang was called "Cool Awesome Chicks", or CAC (which I always thought made them sound like one of the milder swear words for poo).

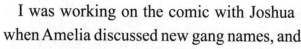

I was working on the comic with Joshua when Amelia discussed new gang names, and when I came back at the end of lunch I discovered that Amelia had settled on: "Great United Friends". Or, as it unfortunately spells out: GUF.

Yep. That's right. *Guf.* Yes, *exactly.* Amelia has learned *nothing* from last term about how acronyms work.

By the time I was able to point out that this made it sound like "guff", a word often taken to mean both "fart" and "nonsense" – neither of which, let's face it, have particularly positive associations – the motion had been passed. (Ha ha, *motion had been passed.*)

Of course, Amelia insists you say it G.U.F., but I think we all know the truth. We could have been called *ACE*, the *idiots*.

Still, it was fun making the new cartoon badges for everyone. (Though I resisted the temptation to draw fart clouds – even though Joshua double-dared me to. And I wrote G.U.F. in *very* tiny lettering.)

Back in class, Natalie leaps to my defence against Amelia's accusation. "Yeah, Amelia, Jess just has a slightly weird face." Thanks, Natalie. Still, at least she *is* defending me though; that is huge progress on last term.

"Hey, Jessica?" We're interrupted by Hannah, a girl in our class.

"Uh, yes," I reply.

"Please can you draw a rabbit on my rough book for me?"

"Oh, yes, sure," I reply happily. Then I address Natalie and Amelia joke-haughtily. "Excuse me a moment, ladies. I have to be a *cartoonist*. We can get back to discussing my weird face afterwards if you like."

Natalie laughs and then looks at me drily, with one eyebrow raised. "You've changed," she says.

I know Nat was joking, but I have *not* changed. Just because I think I'm totally brilliant at cartoons now doesn't mean I've become *arrogant* or anything. *Hmmm.* Still.

And anyway, I think as I walk from the bus stop to my house, *maybe Natalie and Amelia just can't handle it that now* I'm *the awesome, popular one?* Well, kind of. That is to say, *I'm* the one not being *overtly* bullied by the scary kids any more. But again, this is still a huge step up on last term.

But the point is, I haven't changed. It's people's *appreciation* of what I can do that's changed. (There's already a bit of a buzz about the launch of our comic tomorrow – it's going to take Year Six by *storm*.) But I'm exactly the same as I ever was.

And I've always drawn cartoons on people's books for them. Admittedly, it's happening slightly more now, but you know, cartoons have always been my *thing*. It's an open-and-shut case of jealousy, I decide, as I enter my kitchen.

The great thing about home these days is that the economy drive my parents subjected us to last term is over.

"You'll have to put two teabags in there; these Value ones don't taste of anything." My mum is barking instructions at my dad, who is boiling the kettle and hastily putting shopping away.

My Spidey Senses are suddenly tingling. *Value* teabags? I spot that all the rest of the shopping has the same "Super Saver Value" branding on it. *Super Saver Value* tins of tomatoes, *Super Saver Value* squash, *Super Saver Value* cornflakes. I can't help but feel that so many words about saving money in one product name isn't a good thing.

"Hi," I say warily as my mum wrestles the toastie maker out of a junk-filled cupboard. I feel a brief leap of excitement – I *love* cheese toasties! But this excitement is extinguished after a moment of watching my mum impatiently trying to butter some thin-looking *Super Saver Value* bread.

"Hi," she replies absently, the knife going right through the bread and causing several holes.

I mean, I don't claim to be an *expert* on cheese toasties, but I *do* know that's going to make for one messy blob once the cheese melts. I want to point this out, but it's always wise to be careful when giving my mum *constructive criticism*. I'll have to be *tactful*.

"Um, what's with the bread?" I say, a bit untactfully.

"*Don't* start with me!" snaps my mum.

"PPPRRRRAAAAAAAAAASSSSHHH!" This is when my little brother, Ryan, chooses to run into the room with his arms above his head, pretending to be a space rocket.

He's so loud I feel like the house almost shakes. If this was a cartoon, bits of plaster would be falling from the ceiling, nearby dogs would start barking and there'd be a long shot of planet Earth from space, Ryan's voice still audible. As it is, all that happens is my mum's left eye starts twitching a bit.

"*Indoor* voice, please, Ryan," says my dad calmly, as if Ryan has merely spoken a fraction of a decibel too loud.

Ryan stops running with his arms above his head and blinks at my dad in apparent surprise. "But, Daddy, I *can't*, I'm a *space rocket*," he explains, as if my dad's insane, even though he's the one wearing a helmet and thinking he's a space rocket.

"If you don't stop making so much noise you're going to be in big trouble," my dad threatens politely.

"Der Der *Der*!" exclaims Ryan dramatically, making the noise you sometimes hear to indicate a cliffhanger or unexpected twist on a TV show.

Secretly, I find this kind of funny. But I am less keen on how loud Ryan is. He really does tread that delicate line between cute and annoying. I sometimes feel torn between screaming and laughing at him.

10

I know it's not his fault or anything; this is just what six-year-olds do, but *still*. Why can't he do impressions of rockets parked quietly with their engines switched off?

Ryan seems to have got the message though, so I turn my attention back to Mum. "I'm not *starting*," I say carefully, wary of enraging her more than I have to. "But that bread looks too flimsy for cheese toasties. Why didn't you buy the good stuff?"

"Because it's *too expensive*," says my mum crossly.

"But I thought the economy drive was *over*," I protest pointlessly, given the surrounding evidence.

The economy drive was *awful*. My mum refused to buy *any* new food until we had eaten everything that was in the cupboards and freezer. This meant my parents were combining things like fish fingers and tinned beetroot, and calling it dinner.

"The economy drive *is* over," says my dad.

"Then what's all this?" I ask.

"Well…" my dad pauses, thinking, "…now we are *tightening our belts*."

"Der Der *Der*!" says Ryan.

DER DER DER!

Chapter 2

"Um, I don't mean to split hairs," I say carefully, aware my mum is already mildly irked and still not wishing to tip her into full-blown anger, "but that sounds like another way of saying the same thing."

"It's similar," agrees my dad.

"So when you said we were out of the economy drive, what you meant by that was we were in *no way* out of the economy drive?" I continue.

"Did you lie?" asks Ryan, his interest suddenly piqued.

"Don't say lie, say fib," answers my dad. "It's more polite."

"Oh sorry," I reply sarcastically, "so basically you told us a polite but giant, humongous, epic *fib*?"

"No," says my dad. "We are *tightening our belts*. It *is* different. And actually, it's a good chance for you to learn more about fiscal responsibility."

If my dad thinks he can win an argument by using words I don't understand, he is temporarily correct. But I am going to Google that later.

"Why don't you kids do something useful like lay the table?" says my mum.

"Or," I counter, "why don't we just eat with our hands and save on washing-up liquid? Or maybe there's some tasteless cardboard we could eat instead that would be cheaper and less messy than actual food."

My mum is *not* impressed by my sarcasm. "*What* did I tell you about starting with me?" she asks, slamming the butter knife down on the counter.

"Tea!" blurts out my dad. "I've nearly finished making your cup of tea. Hang on." Then in a curt undertone to me he adds, "Jessica, please do as you're told."

"But I thought it was good to speak your mind," I counter cheekily. "Auntie Joan says so."

"Yes, well, Auntie Joan also thinks she's seen Bigfoot," sighs my dad, handing my mum a cup of tea.

I decide to accept that they have won this round and grudgingly start handing cutlery to Ryan.

The thing about my mum is, although she is lovely on the *inside*, she's a bit prone to bursts of anger on the *outside*, unless constantly placated with cups of tea. There's probably a Latin name for this condition. *Anger-tea-icus*, maybe?

In many ways she's actually very laid back. She only gets angry when things are *too expensive*, or *too noisy*, or *too messy*. So the main cause of her affliction is that she lives with us.

Sometimes she gets annoyed by the little things. Like if there's a queue; or someone hasn't put the scissors back; or if my older sister Tammy gets arrested for protesting.

Recently she's been annoyed by the fact that  our car wing-mirror is held on by gaffer tape, while our next-door neighbours (the VanDerks, with whom my parents are weirdly competitive) have been gloating about their new car. She describes stuff like this in particular as the *living end*.

But anyway, as I say, apart from all *that* she's lovely.

So what has two thumbs and got to eat rock-hard, crispy fried-cheese-bread last night for dinner? *This guy.* (You can't see me but I am pointing at myself with my thumbs. Geddit? Sure, I'm recycling, but you've got to keep hold of the gold.)

I didn't mind really; it still tasted nice. And overall I like my life at the moment. As they say, tomorrow is another day.

Well, actually, tomorrow is today. What I mean is, it is the next day. Today, now. You know what I mean. Basically it's Wednesday. I'm in my form room at registration pretending to be interested in Natalie and Amelia's list of their top-five favourite pop stars.

YAY!

But more important than any of that, it's *comic-launch-day*! I briefly wonder how famous you'd have to be to actually rename a day of the week like that. (I definitely haven't changed, though. Definitely.)

I looked up "fiscal responsibility" online last night, after dinner. It brought up loads of stuff about economics and governments and treasuries, but, as far as I could tell, "fiscal" essentially just means financial, so it's all to do with money.

Why didn't my dad just say we need to be careful with money? He can dress it up in fancy words if he likes, but I am from the Google generation and we can easily decipher them. (As long as we have the Internet handy.) We coped with no money before; we can cope again. I just wish they'd be honest about it.

I should totally write a "parents' handbook" or something.

Hey, maybe that would be a funny idea for the comic! But the bell goes before I get a chance to write it down.

Stupid assembly, making me lose my creative flow, I think sulkily as we file into the big hall.

"What's up with you?" whispers Natalie as we stop at the end of our row.

"Oh nothing, I just – hey, you don't have a pen on you, do you?" I whisper back. Maybe I could quickly write this on the back of the hymn sheet!

"Um, let me think…" Nat pretends to pat non-existent pockets, looking for a pen. "Uh, *no*." She frowns at me quizzically.

"That's cool, I was just going to write down an idea. I – it doesn't matter," I whisper, suddenly feeling slightly embarrassed. Natalie and Amelia just don't get how brilliant the comic is, and so they don't care about it as much as I do.

"God, I'm getting, like, *so* bored of your tortured artist routine," whispers Amelia, and Natalie giggles, which annoys me.

Oh yeah? *Well, I'm getting bored of your face*, I think. And *what* tortured artist routine? I am a *happy* artist. I don't say anything though, and probably for the best. I can come up with better zingers than that.

There is a notice in assembly that all of Year Six are having an *extra* assembly after lunch in the hall.

But I don't care about whatever that is. The main event as far as I'm concerned is our comic launch at lunchtime. Even Amelia insulting me doesn't bother me for long today. I'm too excited.

I can't *wait* for my morning lessons of double English and double DT to be over. Which in many ways is a shame, as I like DT, and I don't really mind English, but I just can't concentrate.

My friends Cherry and Shantair actually tell me to shut up about the comic in DT (which is kind of impressive in itself because they are my chess-club friends and they're normally too shy to do stuff like that). But they like getting good marks and I was distracting them.

Luckily they're not grudge-holders and we're all friends again by the end of the lesson. And Shantair has still consented to the use of her hair ribbon in our comic opening ceremony at lunch.

My friends Emily, Megan and Fatimah are more excited. They're my friends who like messing around and hate working hard. They kept nudging me in DT and giving me "thumbs-up" signs, which

I think might have been part of what was annoying Cherry and Shantair.

I don't sit with Natalie in these lessons because we all got moved around at the start of Year Six and she ended up next to Amelia.

Every now and then in DT, I catch Joshua's eye across the room and grin. I think we both feel a bit nervous, but pleased.

Joshua is my newest friend. All this year I sat next to him in art but apart from when I brilliantly introduced the Would You Rather? game in one lesson, he didn't really talk to me that much.

Then, when I fell out with Natalie, I ended up hanging out with my other friends more, and, well – long story short – we discovered we both love cartoons. Starting the comic was his idea.

Finally the bell goes for lunch. My stomach flips over. It's *showtime*!

Chapter 3

"I now declare the *Hell*fern Comic open!" booms Tanya Harris, and she cuts Shantair's ribbon that has been tied round Issue One. Our eight spectators in 6C clap politely. Natalie, Amelia, Shantair, Cherry, Megan, Emily and Fatimah (basically the ACE half of GUF). Also Harriet VanDerk is here, to "check we do it properly".

"Now!" instructs Tanya, and on cue Lewis and I pull the strings on two party poppers, mainly emptying the contents over Tanya's and Joshua's heads. Emily does that whistle with her fingers in her mouth that I can't do. I manage to resist the urge to shout, "Ta daaaa!"

The comic is *beautiful*, in my opinion. It's not very long, just one piece of A4 folded in half. It's all been printed out on Lewis's dad's fancy printer (without him knowing).

The front cover is one of my now-famous sheep cartoons. This time, it's of our French teacher, Miss Price. In the cartoon a pupil is choking and just manages to squeak, "Call an ambulance!" Miss Price then replies, "Only if you say it in French!"

(Miss Price is very insistent we speak only French in her lessons. She sometimes won't even let people go to the toilet until they say it in French. This means we sometimes learn more about miming French than speaking French, but I guess mime did *originate* in France, so it's still kind of on-topic.)

Page Two, also known as the inside cover, is a quiz that Tanya and I came up with together, called "Which EastEnders Character Are You?" It's a spoof of one of those box quizzes you get in magazines, where you follow the arrows depending on your answers.

The question boxes in this one say things like, "Have you ever walked into the Old Vic and said 'Woz goin' on?'?" If you say "YES," you follow the arrow to the answer: "You're that one that shouts all the time,"; if you say "NO," then you go to "You're that one that cries all the time."

Page Three, inside the back cover, is an original comic strip by Joshua and Lewis. It's called "Roland the Slightly Rubbish Superhero" and I think it's great. Roland is a bit stronger than a normal man, but not enough to lift a car off a trapped person. And he can hear through walls, but not enough to know what the bad guys are actually saying; he can just make out vague words. As a result, his crime fighting is average.

The fourth and final page, which is also the back

cover, is a collection of spoof news and spoof gossip about our school. Things like "Which teacher was spotted going into the staffroom with bogeys hanging from their nose?" We all contributed to this one. It was so much fun coming up with stupid and crazy things the teachers might have been doing.

It was also when doing this page that we realised our comic must NEVER be seen by any teachers, EVER. It must be kept hidden from them at all costs. We just don't think they'd see the funny side, somehow.

"Speech! Speech!" calls out Megan.

"Actually, they don't normally *have* speeches at comic book launches," chips in Harriet VanDerk.

"How can you possibly know that?" I ask her tiredly. But she just smiles smugly instead of answering.

"Whatever," says Tanya, leaning against our desks

in 6C. "Tanya Harris ain't doing no speeches. This is showbiz, not nerdbiz."

Harriet wisely doesn't question this. (I assume more because she's scared of Tanya Harris than because she's been blown away by the showbiz nature of us cutting a hair ribbon and letting off two party poppers.)

I thought we might have gone too far with the party poppers actually (especially as we're trying to keep it secret from teachers) but Tanya really wanted the *razzle dazzle*. And basically you don't argue with Tanya Harris. I mean, you *can*, but if you do, you need to: (a) know where the exits are, and (b) pick your battles wisely.

Tanya can be *really* naughty. Or at least she used to be. It seems gone are the days when she spat in Mrs Cole's face (and got suspended for it), or when she keyed Mr Denton's car (and got suspended for it). And she hasn't even put chewing gum in anyone's hair for ages now. (Which will be a huge relief to Amelia because she was

24

the main victim of that. Tanya thought Amelia was too snooty, which she was, but *still*.)

Some people might think Tanya sounds like an unusual choice of person to go into business with. But I say *this* to those people: "You are right, actually." And in fact Lewis *did* make that very point at our first official comic meeting.

What happened was this. It was the end of last term, nearly the Easter holidays, and Natalie and I had just become best friends again. I'd gone to the library to meet Joshua and his friend, Lewis, with some of my rough comic ideas sketched out.

We'd been discussing all the different things we could do, when the subject of the comic's name came up. Joshua had an idea. He said, "I think we should call it—"

"*Hell*fern Juniors!" Tanya had dramatically barged into the Quiet Reading Area, interrupting us.

Joshua and Lewis expressed surprise to see her, and Tanya explained that "a little birdie" had told her we were planning on starting a comic with "her idea" and it was "bare jokes" that we thought

25

we could steal it from her.

Joshua argued and said even if he *did* want to call the comic that, it was just a funny name. And then Tanya was *really* livid. She said, "In case you forgot, our school ain't called *Hell*fern, it's called *Hill*fern. I said our school was like Hell and told Toons here –" she gestured at me then, "– to draw a cartoon of it, and call it *Hell*fern. That's mine."

(Tanya calls me Toons because I draw – geddit? Well, don't shoot the messenger.)

This was true. Tanya *had* told me to draw the *Hell*fern cartoon of our school when she was annoyed she'd been "stitched up" and given a detention. I drew the building on fire with slightly scary lettering proclaiming it "*Hell*fern Juniors". Tanya had loved it so much, she photocopied it and put it all round school.

"All right, so you came up with a joke," said Joshua.

"Yeah. So that's *mine*," said Tanya.

"It's not yours,"

26

protested Lewis.

"It *is*," said Tanya. Then, "I've been watching *Law And Order*, and that name is my *intellectual property*."

There was a moment of silence as it sunk in that not only had Tanya just won this argument, but that the scariest girl in our school had just used the legal term "intellectual property".

Prior to that I think if people had ever pictured Tanya interacting with the law, it had probably been in the capacity of criminal rather than prosecutor. (But I think, if anything, this highlights how unfair some reputations are.)

Joshua looked resigned. "All right, Tanya, so what do you want from us?" he asked.

"I want *in*," said Tanya.

I felt like I was in a film. I never thought I would be party to a conversation at school where someone actually got to use the phrase "*I want in*", and I was in a gang last term and everything.

Disappointingly, the others had been oblivious to my secret delight. They all seemed pretty serious. I nearly tried to lighten the mood by joking that, at this rate, we'd all be jumping in taxis and shouting,

"Follow that car!"
But it didn't seem
like the right time.

The argument
continued for a
bit. Lewis said something about not thinking
it was a "good fit". Tanya said something about Lewis
losing his attitude "by going home in an ambulance".

I think, logistically, Lewis knew that he
wouldn't be going *home* in an ambulance,
he'd (if anything) be going to hospital in one.
But probably Tanya's use of the word "ambulance"
was enough to make him take the threat seriously
and not bother to point this out to her.

Joshua had tried a different tack. "Look, the thing
is, we've already got enough people," he said.

Then the inevitable happened.

"Says who?" said Tanya. "Toons wants me in,
don't you, Toons?"

They all turned and looked at me. I wondered if this
would be the bit in the film where the really awesome
girl called Jessica would be unfairly set upon because
she couldn't please everyone. Because, personally, I
thought that film would go *straight* to DVD.

But as they were looking at me, I realised that I *did* want Tanya in the comic. Sure, on the one hand she still kind of terrified me, but she had also been a loyal friend when I fell out with Natalie and Amelia (if anything, maybe a bit too loyal). And she had actually been quite instrumental in the whole cartoons thing taking off.

I mean, she'd not only been coming up with funny rude ideas to draw, but she'd also been distributing them around school and finding us an audience. It would seem crazy to stop her helping us do that, to my mind.

Lewis took some convincing. I tried to explain about Tanya's creative and distribution skills as best I could. I suspected that part of the problem was that Lewis and Joshua were worried Tanya can be a bully, so I tried to make this look like a good thing.

"You want to charge for the comic and make money, don't you? You know, eventually, once we're established? Well, no one's going to refuse to pay Tanya, are they?"

"Well…" Joshua looked like he was considering this.

"Look, I know you guys are worried about her

reputation, or that she'll take over," I continued.

"*Oi!*" said Tanya.

"But it's like … it's like – you're thinking of Tanya like she's Batman," I said triumphantly, pleased I could get my point across by speaking their language, the language of comic books.

"Sorry, *how*?" asked Joshua, folding his arms but looking vaguely amused. He'd raised one eyebrow, in a *this better be good* type way.

"You think Tanya is the hero *Hell*fern deserves but not the one it needs right now," I said.

"No, I don't." Joshua looked a bit like he was trying not to laugh. "Sorry, but it's not like Batman. I don't think— Tanya is not like Batman." He glanced nervously at her. "No offence, Tanya."

"None taken," replied Tanya amicably. (I think, by this point, she had started enjoying all this discussion about her. And being compared to Batman.)

"It doesn't even slightly work in this context," continued Joshua.

"Anyway," I steered things back, "whatever you think, Tanya has a nice side that not many people see. Don't misjudge her … Tanya is funny … and loyal … and … and actually has the soul of a poet." (OK, even I wasn't sure where I'd got that from.)

"Yeah," said Tanya. "*And* I'll punch anyone that doesn't pay up." (Which I think slightly stepped on my poetry point. Unless you count war poetry – that's quite violent.)

But Tanya was in. Lewis was overruled. And practically overnight Tanya ended her reign of terror as the naughtiest girl in our school and started to focus more on her *business* career.

Back at the launch, Nat whispers, "I'm so proud of you," and she squeezes my arm. "You're a published cartoonist now!"

I beam at her. I mean, really, I'm a *self*-published cartoonist, but what she said sounds better.

A surge of pleasure shoots through me. We *did*

this. We did it! It's *our* cartoon comic. And this is just the *beginning*. I feel like we're on an amazing adventure and we have a voice. I suddenly feel full of happiness and excitement at the thought. I squeeze Natalie's arm back.

I never realised how important self-expression was to me until I finally had an outlet for it. Because now if anything bad happens to me, I can just turn it into a cartoon and feel better. Ever since I drew that sheep of Amelia, I feel like things can't get to me as much. *What's that, Mum? I'm grounded? Well, you might just find yourself on the wrong side of a cartoon!* Ha ha.

See? I definitely haven't gone mad with power, or changed.

"Thanks," I reply. Natalie and Amelia do seem genuinely impressed. They love events and planning and stuff, so I guess they are in their element at a launch.

"And don't forget," says Natalie, "I'm your biggest fan, and I knew you before all this. So don't go thinking you can sack me off now just because you're famous." She sounds jokey but there's something serious about her eyes.

I can't help but laugh. "*Famous?* Nat, have you even *seen* how many people are here? Do you want me to do a head count?" (I've actually already done one – it's eight. We have eight fans. But that's not the point. I'm being self-deprecating, and that proves I haven't changed.)

Natalie splutters laughter. "You know what I mean."

It's probably a good thing most of Year Six are outside, actually. Too many more people might have attracted the attention of a teacher.

"Don't worry," I say. "Best friends forever," and I take out my half of our broken-heart necklace. She takes her half out and we match them up so they say

"Best Friends Forever" on them. We both smile. She relaxes, though I have to say, I think it's a bit rich that Nat could complain at all, considering how  she went off with Amelia last term and everything.

"What on EARTH is going on in here?"

I look up, startled. Mrs Cole is standing at the entrance to 6C, looking angry.

Chapter 4

Oh *nooo*! I freeze in panic as a cold chill grips my neck. "*Please don't see the comics, please don't see the comics*," I repeat helplessly, on a loop in my head. What should I do? What should I do?

Surely I should probably do *something*?

Nooooo!

But before I can do anything, Tanya swiftly and calmly throws her coat over the pile of comics on the desk and turns to address Mrs Cole. "What's up, teach?"

"Tanya, do not call me 'teach'. Please address me as Mrs Cole or Miss. And what's up is that it's a lovely sunny day and I don't understand why such a large group of you are indoors."

"Well, Miss, we were going to throw you a surprise party, but you've ruined it now," says Tanya, completely unflappable in the presence of a teacher.

"All right, let's make this even easier, shall we?" says Mrs Cole wearily. "Get outside now, all of you, and you won't have to come and see me at the end of school and tell me what's really been going on. Go on. Out. Now."

She holds the form-room door open for us, waiting, as we all file past. Tanya scoops up her coat and the comics, turning it into a kind of scrunched-up basket.

"I don't think you need your coat outside today, Tanya," says Mrs Cole. My heart starts beating even faster. I'm worried I'm bright red and completely giving the game away.

"Actually I do, Miss," says Tanya, unfazed. "My mum says I'm not to let this coat out of my sight because if I lose it she will beat me from one end of the school to the other. Bit over the top, isn't it, Miss? Do you think I should phone ChildLine?"

"OK, Tanya, just go." Mrs Cole rolls her eyes and looks tired as she closes the door behind us, then heads back to the staffroom.

No one speaks until we are all the way outside.

"Oh my God! Tanya, you were amazing!" Emily pats Tanya on the back.

"I can't believe you said those things to Mrs Cole!" exclaims Megan.

"You saved our bacon," agrees Joshua. Even Lewis looks impressed.

I don't want to say *I told you so* to Lewis, so I just give him my new raised-eyebrow smug look (that I've been practising in the mirror to annoy Ryan). I'm pretty sure Tanya's position on the team is now assured forever. Although she is in some ways a beacon for teacher suspicion and interference, she's also a master of subterfuge, so it evens out.

"Nice one!" I tell her.

"Cosmic," replies Tanya.

I smile uncertainly. "Uh, cosmic?"

"It's retro, innit?" says Tanya. "I'm bringing it back. Pass it on."

"What do you think this is all about?" whispers Natalie as we file into the hall after lunch for our extra assembly.

"I don't know," I whisper back, trying not to yawn. I'm not that curious about it. "Road safety lecture?"

Once we're all assembled in the hall, Miss Price addresses us from the front. "Well, everyone, I suppose you're wondering why we've brought you here."

I have to fight the urge to shout, "No! Not really!" Then I have to fight the urge not to giggle. Maybe hanging out with Joshua and Tanya and trying to come **SNIGGER** up with rude things to say *is* starting to affect me?

Miss Price continues, unaware that I have silently dissed her. "We have some very exciting news."

I'll be the judge of that, I think. Ha ha.

"As you know, nature is all around us. It is fascinating and complex, and it is very important…" (I try and stifle another yawn.) "Therefore, we are very pleased to announce the Year Six Wildlife Project!"

I look at Natalie. She smiles. "*Not* a road safety lecture then."

Miss Price continues, "We've gone to a lot of trouble to liaise with local authorities to ensure that instead of some normal lessons, you will go on some really interesting field trips as part of your research experience."

"This sounds all right, you know," whispers Natalie.

"Maybe," I whisper back. I mean, *field trips* sound all right. "Especially if we get to miss geography and stuff more than art," I add. Yeah, maybe this could be *fun*.

"And," says Miss Price, "as there is an even number of you in the whole year, what we'd like you to do is get into pairs."

Then again... *Noooooo!*

I feel like someone's just poured a bucket of cold water over my head. It's splashing everywhere, destroying the life I once knew, that I tried so hard to rebuild. (OK, maybe that's a *tad* dramatic, but still.)

Great. Well, this is just *great.* Now Natalie has to choose between Amelia and me, *again.* And Amelia is still kind of the new girl, so Nat will probably feel she has to choose her, *again.* Then they'll spend all this enforced extra time together, there will be a new batch of *in-jokes* that I don't get, and before you know it I'll be out in the cold. *Again.*

What's *wrong* with our school? Why can't we go in groups of *three* or something? Why would you do this to me, Universe? *Why?* Remember when we had that discussion, and we agreed that I was brilliant and that only good things should happen to me from now on? Well, I kept up my end (being brilliant) so thanks a bunch.

The French have this saying: *plus ça change.* It means "nothing ever changes" or something along those lines. I'm not exactly sure that's the whole thing – I'd needed the toilet in that lesson so I was distracted but it seems totally true to me right now.

My family were *supposed* to be off the economy drive, and now we're *tightening our belts*, which is nearly the same thing. Natalie and Amelia promised *never* to go off without me again. And now fate has found a way to make it happen all over again. *Nothing ever really changes in this stupid place*, I think angrily.

I'm just kind of standing there, inwardly wincing and looking at the floor. I don't want to see Natalie's apologetic face. Or Amelia's smug one. Right. OK. I can be dignified in defeat. Definitely. Probably. I just need to remember how to do my fake smile. *Ohhh*.

Natalie nudges my arm gently. "Do you want to be my partner?" she whispers. *What?*

"W-what?" I whisper back.

"*WHAT?*" echoes Amelia, in what I might have to describe as shock.

"If you don't want to go with Joshua or Cherry or Tanya or anyone?" adds Natalie. No way! Joshua is great, and I do like Cherry and Tanya, but Natalie is my *best* friend.

"No, I'd *love* to go with you!" I whisper, elated.

"Yay!" whispers Natalie.

41

"Quieten down! Quieten down!" shouts Miss Price. The noise in the hall has risen steadily from a murmur to a hubbub. People are chattering and pointing at each other across the room.

I can't believe Natalie chose *me*. ME. This is brilliant. Everything is brilliant again. It's going to be just like the old days, hanging out all the time, having fun – us against the world! And hopefully, as Amelia's influence lessens, there won't be as much admin.

BEST FRIEND

Maybe this whole term is going to be brilliant after all!

Maybe the French are wrong about *plus ça change*. I mean, they're wrong about thinking it's a good idea to eat frogs' legs. I imagine.

42

Chapter 5

"What do you *mean* it's not too late for Nat to change her mind?" I repeat Amelia's audacious suggestion more out of shock than a desire for her to repeat it.

(I'm sorry, France – you were right all along. I should have known things never change. And I bet frogs *are* delicious.)

We should be in French but instead it's the first ever lesson of the wildlife project. We're in the DT classroom because it's bigger and the desks are wider for project planning. We're sorting out our groups and being given literature and work sheets on the subject and stuff. It turns out it's

43

quite a full-on project.

Other people have asked to go in bigger groups as they are having trouble deciding between friends. But Miss Price has explained that they want us to really learn about teamwork, and that sometimes in bigger groups, certain members can get away with "coasting" while the others do the work. But in groups of two that's not really possible so everyone has to pull their weight.

Amelia has just brazenly walked up to Natalie and said Nat could still go in a two with her. Unbelievable.

"Look, I'm not saying this to be horrible," lies Amelia. "But Natalie and I are a better *fit*. We work the same way, and we already sit next to each other in most lessons."

"Hey, Jess," says Joshua, approaching at that moment. "Are you in a two already?"

"Uh…" Can I say *yes*? What if Nat has just changed her mind? "Well, I *was* going to go with Natalie."

"Oh, no worries. I'll go with Lewis." He disappears again.

If Natalie is about to reject me, I wonder how undignified it will look if I run after Joshua and say I want to go with him after all? *Hmmm.*

"Look, Amelia—" begins Nat, but she is interrupted by Tanya Harris.

"Tooooons!" She claps me on the back, then she clocks who I'm standing with. "Natalie. Lady Muck." She nods at them. "Toons, wanna go with me for the project?"

Hmmm. Do I? It would probably be quite fun to go with Tanya, actually. We'd spend most of the time coming up with rude things for the comic. And I like Tanya. Especially since I'm hardly even scared of her any more.

"Come *on*!" she barks, and I jump slightly. (*See?* In the olden days I would have jumped *much* further. We've really come a long way.)

"I was going to go with Nat," I say, still unsure if this is the case.

"No, don't go with her, go with me. We'll have loads of fun together."

"I think that's a good idea," says Amelia unexpectedly (she's normally too scared of Tanya Harris to talk in front of her). "I think you two are a *good fit*." Amelia raises an eyebrow deliberately at me.

45

"Well, no one cares what *you* think," snaps Tanya, annoyed at being agreed with by someone she has previously called a "posh cow".

"Look, sorry everyone, but Jess and I have already agreed to go together," pipes up Natalie bravely. (She's also been known to get on the wrong side of Tanya Harris, and doesn't want to antagonise her.)

"Fair dos, fair dos," says Tanya amicably. "Laters." And she disappears off again.

"Amelia, I'm sorry, but I'm going with Jess," says Nat kindly. "I didn't do much with her last term, and like you said, we already sit together, so I'll still see you loads."

"Well, OK," sighs Amelia. "*Your* funeral." (What's that supposed to mean?)

"What's that supposed to mean?" asks Natalie.

"Well, just, obviously if you did want to go with me and *get a good grade*, now is the time to say so, and Jessica can go with one of these … people she's more academically suited to."

OK, that's a pretty unsubtle way of calling me

stupid. And my friends. I mean, sure, Tanya isn't exactly known for her grades, but Joshua does well at most things.

I know the real reason Amelia doesn't like Joshua. And it's not just that he's my friend so she feels obliged to dislike him. It's because he likes science fiction. Well, him and Lewis together.

At the end of last term Amelia and Natalie were desperate to organise an outing with the boys from the basketball team, so they kept begging me to get Joshua to set it up. I didn't want to tell Joshua so overtly that they only wanted his "cool" basketball team friends, so Joshua invited Lewis.

We ended up, the five of us, round at Natalie's house, watching Lewis's favourite film because he took them at their word that they wanted to watch DVDs (whereas Natalie and Amelia had hoped the subtext – that they wanted to play Truth Or Dare and stuff – might shine through).

So we ended up watching the first *Star Wars* film, "A New Hope". It was made in the 1970s and I thought it stood up pretty well. I really enjoyed it. But Amelia hated it. Natalie half liked it, but the main thing we all noticed about it was how much all the characters overused the phrase "delusions of grandeur" to insult each other.

Amelia has gone off the idea of setting up any more boy-outings through me or Joshua since then.

I'm annoyed Amelia thinks she can slyly call me an idiot. I don't care if she *is* just jealous or insecure, it's still uncalled for. I know I should just rise above it, but at the same time there's some things you probably shouldn't let go, otherwise people will walk all over you.

"Amelia, if you've got something to say, just say it. Do you think I'm not clever enough to go with Natalie or something?" I ask her.

"Well, if the cap fits," says Amelia primly. My annoyance shoots up further. She's so *smug*! And I'm doing all the legwork here, just to establish that I have indeed been insulted.

I will myself not to respond, but for some reason my mouth still says, "*Yeah?* Well, I'm very fun and popular, maybe *that's* why Natalie wants to go with me. Not everything is about getting top marks, you know."

"Clearly," retorts Amelia.

I instantly regret saying this. It's dangerous territory and I know it. (a) I'm not very fun and popular, and (b) this project *is* about getting top marks.

Amelia sighs. "Look, I intend to come top of the class in this project, babes. I was great at stuff like this at my old school. Honestly, it's cool though. No hard feelings."

"Well, we don't care about getting high marks!" I counter, my voice going worryingly shrill. "We just want to hang out and have the most fun we possibly can while doing this project!"

"Well, we do want to get high marks *as well*," says Natalie, looking – if I'm totally honest here – a *tad* worried. But only for a second. Then she links her arm through mine and addresses Amelia defiantly. "We're going to do *both*."

"Yeah!" I say.

Amelia does her best to look bored and unimpressed at the same time. "If you say so," she replies. Then she adds, "Good *luck*," in a really sarcastic voice and stalks off.

Chapter 6

"Wouldn't it be great if we actually *beat* her?" says Natalie as we select DT desks, sit down and start unpacking our wildlife project literature.

"Yeah!" I say sceptically. "But that's not what's important though, is it?"

"Oh no, of course not!" says Nat quickly. "I am *so* excited we're doing our project together!" She turns over the first page of one of the information handouts.

"I know! It's going to be great!" I agree.

"It's going to be a lot of hours, and extra homework and stuff," says Natalie, "but what a brilliant excuse to go round to each other's houses!"

"Exactly!" I grin. "I mean, I *hate* your house,

with all its delicious food and comfy sofas, but I am prepared to make that sacrifice for the greater good."

Nat chuckles and I start leafing through some of the work sheets as well. Some of it looks kind of interesting. It's a lot to take in in one go though; it's kind of a bit daunting. I don't say this.

"It would be good to get started right away," says Natalie. "Why don't you come round to mine tonight? We can get a head start, go through the rest of the information pack together?"

"Oh, well actually, it's Wednesday. I have chess club right after school."

"Oh," says Nat, and her face falls a bit.

The chess club has been a small bone of contention between Nat and me in the past, as she thinks it takes up a lot of my time. That's partly one of the reasons why she went off with Amelia. I mean, it's all sorted now and everything. But, you know, it's *typical* for the project to get announced on the *one* day I have an after-school commitment. (Not counting the ace comic, but I can do that any time.)

I like being in the chess club. Even though I used to get, well, not exactly *bullied* for it, but there was a bit of name-calling. Except I'm not sure you can even call it name-calling. Some of the mean boys used to say, "Ooh, chess club" as I walked past sometimes. I mean, I know that's not exactly a rude insult on its own, but it was the *way* they said it.

Then Tanya Harris got really excited about a picture I drew of her as a Cadbury Creme Egg and showed it to everyone, and they all stopped doing it. (This is another one of the reasons I'm really glad the cartoons thing is working out; it's made me far more accepted than I previously was.)

"Well, what about tomorrow night?" I suggest quickly.

"Oh yes, definitely, tomorrow night," agrees Natalie. "We don't want to get too far behind."

"Jeez, Nat, chill out. It's just a wildlife project. We're all supposed to work at our own speed and stuff."

"Well, Jess – and I say this with love – I think we should try to work slightly faster than your 'own speed and stuff'," says Natalie.

"Ouch," I say and pull a mock-offended face. "Well, sorreeeee."

Natalie giggles. "You know what I mean."

"So you agree with Amelia?"

"No, but, come *on*.
You remember 'Egypt'."

Oh, it is so unfair of her to bring
that up. I'm a totally different person now. OK,
so last year when we had to do a project on Egypt, I
might have got slightly carried away with drawing all
the mummies and sphinxes and *ever so slightly* run
out of time for the actual writing, and come bottom
of the class.

"Nat—" I begin.

"And 'The Amazon'?" she interrupts. OK, a
similar thing happened the year before, when I drew
too many parrots for the project on the Amazon
rainforest. "See?" says Nat. "There's a pattern
developing here."

Hmmm. I don't know about a *pattern*
exactly. But OK, so maybe I do have
a *slight* track record of drawing
excellent pictures for projects
and not working quite hard
enough on the writing. "All right."
I sigh in recognition. "I drew some
brilliant parrots though. You said so
yourself."

Natalie laughs. "Oh yes, they were second to none," she says. "You're such a weirdo."

I laugh.

"But you're *my* weirdo," she adds fondly.

But after the eighth time Nat says we ought to make a timetable for the project – "really get across the whole thing" – it's me who's starting to wonder if this is a huge mistake.

Don't get me wrong, it's not that I don't love Nat. I *do*, she's my best friend. Obviously I love her. *Obviously*. But at the same time, oh-my-God-I-am-already-sick-of-how-seriously-she's-taking-this-project. I can't tell if it's Amelia getting her all competitive, or if this would have happened anyway.

Also (and again, I'm not sure how much of this is because Amelia drew attention to the grades I usually attract) I seem to have been cast as "lovable idiot who doesn't get things", a role which I'm not sure I'm happy to play any more.

That's the Jessica of *last* term. Who wasn't understood by everyone, and had to beg for scraps of Natalie's time when Amelia was busy.

But *now* I am a celebrated *cartoonist*. I am the co-author of a comic. *This* Jessica has other friends. I mean, hello? *Two* whole other people asked to be my partner for this project. I don't have to sit around waiting for Nat to pick me. I don't have to be *Nat's weirdo* any more. I can be *my own* weirdo. (That still doesn't sound that great, actually, but you get my point.)

As Nat makes a list of what we need to do first, I glance around the room and watch Joshua and Lewis deep in discussion, and Tanya laughing her head off at something, and I wonder, for the first time, if I *had* gone with them whether things mightn't have been a lot more fun.

I arrive home later on to find my dad sitting at the kitchen table reading the paper, and my mum boiling some *Super Saver Value* veg and trying to chop garlic, but the garlic seems to keep slipping out of her hand.

"And Horace King has a new programme about bird sanctuaries," my dad announces absently, not looking up from the paper.

"I'm getting really annoyed with this," says my mum crossly. I can't tell if she means the slippery garlic or my dad's pronouncements from the paper.

"Oh sorry," he says. "Would you like a hand?" He stands up. "Oh hello, Jessica, how was school?"

"Oh no, don't worry," says my mum sarcastically. "Just let *muggins here* do everything. *As per usual.*"

Lately I've noticed my mum seems to be trying to start her own nickname. She's always going on about *muggins* or *muggins here*. I'm hoping it's just a phase and she'll grow out of it. I know you're supposed to let them live their own lives and make their own decisions, but I also don't want to feel like I'm colluding in establishing a stupid name. For a start, you're not meant to give *yourself* a nickname. Otherwise everyone would be called AceHead or Mr Fantastico.

"Well then, how about a nice cup of tea?" says my dad, heading for the safety of the kettle and getting some cups out.

"Don't forget to put two teabags in," says my mum.

Suddenly the back door swings open. "You won't *believe* what those VanDerks have said now!" My older sister Tammy bursts into the kitchen, with some paper in one hand and a big bin liner in the other.

The VanDerks are our next-door neighbours and they … well, how can I put this? They're *better* than us. I mean, if you care about having good lawns, and good children and stuff, (which unfortunately my parents do).

I think we have much better personalities though. And *that's* saying something. But my parents aren't satisfied with that; they keep trying to compete in this petty one-upmanship that they deny exists if you try to talk to them about it.

The main downside for me is that Harriet VanDerk is in my year at school, she's a genius at maths and stuff, and she always hands her work in on time. So she gives my parents unhelpful and unrealistic expectations.

Ryan comes running in. "Hi, Tammy! Mummy, did you know there's no Kit Kats left?"

"Hi," says Tammy, deflated that no one has invited

her to continue her story.

"Yes. And there won't be any more for a little while, I'm afraid," says my mum.

"But we *need* them!" Ryan seems astonished.

Not wanting to be sidelined by the necessity or otherwise of Kit Kats, Tammy tries again. "*Look.* I asked them to sign a petition about pollution and they refused!"

"I hope you've not been upsetting the neighbours," says my mum.

"What's a petition?" asks Ryan.

"Oh, I'm sorry." Tammy addresses my mum sarcastically. "Is it an inconvenient time to *safeguard the planet*? God, you're as bad as them. Smug Middle England marches on, eh?"

My dad looks baffled. "I don't know what you're talking about, Tammy, but we're about to have dinner," he says.

I do love my sister Tammy. But she has tended to be a bit *antagonistic* lately. It's not like anyone in our family disagrees with her stance about fighting injustice and looking after the environment and stuff. The conflict mainly arises because my parents would rather do it quietly and (ideally) after the six o'clock news.

Tammy checks out my dad's tea-making. "Are you using two tea bags?" she asks. "Way to rip through the world's resources, guys!"

"They're Value tea bags," I say.

"What's a petition?" repeats Ryan.

"Well then, Value tea bags are a false economy," snaps Tammy, "which I think perfectly exemplifies this family's love of short-term gains and its refusal to look at the big picture."

"Tammy!" shouts Ryan, sick of being ignored.

Tammy crouches down on one knee so she is level with Ryan. "Sorry, Ry," she says. "A petition is when lots of people sign a piece of paper to say they agree something should change. If I get enough signatures, the people causing the pollution will have to do something about it. It's important to take positive action if you believe in something."

Ryan nods seriously. "Can I sign it?" he says.

"No, sorry, you're too young," says Tammy, standing up again.

"Nooo! I want to sign it!" objects Ryan. "I think pollution is bad. Please!"

"No, Ryan, you're under eighteen and you can't vote," Tammy explains unhelpfully, before turning to my parents. "I need the washing machine," she says.

"Well, I need a new wing mirror," says my mum. "Sometimes we don't always get what we want."

Ryan's wailing is in danger of becoming full-scale crying. He's often cranky before a meal.

"Shhh, Ryan! Hang on," I say. "Tammy, could you just let him *sign* it?" I try and do a gesture of inverted commas around the word *sign* without Ryan seeing. "You know, in *pencil*?"

Tammy gets my drift. "Oh, *fine*," she sighs. Ryan instantly stops whingeing and delightedly scrawls 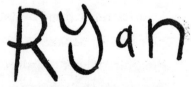 his name in massive letters across half the page. I'm pretty much a genius at solving problems when they involve Ryan or the Internet. No one thanks me for stopping his noise though.

Tammy starts loading clothes from her bin liner into our washing machine. "Did we say she could do that?" My dad is addressing my mum.

"Look," says Tammy. "Don't make me go through the whole thing again. Our student washing machine broke and my flatmates replaced it with one from a company that doesn't pay its UK tax. I refuse to be a part of that. Will you please just support me for once?"

No one physically stops Tammy from using our washing machine though, so she just carries on. "I might as well stay for dinner, while I'm waiting for it," she explains, and starts laying the table.

My parents don't object to this either, and (possibly because she's thinking of her washing) Tammy doesn't start any fights with them over dinner. She doesn't even mention the rescue dog she keeps trying to make them adopt – which is a shame,

 as I would *love* a rescue dog.

We have a relatively normal (for us) dinner, in fact. I tell my parents about the Year Six Wildlife Project, and how I get to go with Natalie, and how it might be exciting. And Ryan talks about what he thinks the merits of space food are. Before Tammy leaves my parents even sign her petition.

Look at *us,* all happy families. Something about it makes me uneasy. Like something must be about to go terribly wrong. Which is crazy. I've got to stop being suspicious about everything, just because it's all going really well at the moment. I am a brilliant cartoonist, Natalie is my partner on the project and we are going to have *fun*. None of that is asking for trouble. None of it.

Chapter 7

"Hi, Nat, guess what?" I say, bounding into my form room on Thursday morning. "My mum says I can come to your house after school tonight!" I stop mid-gush as I clock Natalie's unimpressed face and spot Tanya Harris sitting on my desk, waiting for me.

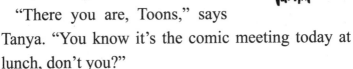

"There you are, Toons," says Tanya. "You know it's the comic meeting today at lunch, don't you?"

"Uh, yeah," I reply uneasily. Why is Natalie frowning?

"Your mate says you're working on the wildlife

project instead." Tanya gestures at Nat. Oh, *that's* why. Triffic.

"Oh dear," says Amelia, eavesdropping. "Not spreading yourself too thin, are you, Jessica?" *Stop stirring!* I want to shout at her.

"*No*," I respond, and then address Nat. "I'm sorry, Nat. It *is* the comic meeting today. But I can come to your house tonight after school, so that's pretty good right?"

"Yeah, I guess." Natalie looks like she's forgetting about being annoyed and unfolds her arms. She smiles at me. "That's cool." Phew. Crisis averted. *In your* face, *Amelia!*

"And we've got ten minutes till registration. We can have a quick look at it now," I add, just as Tanya hands me a small pile of *Hell*fern comics.

"Right then," she says. "I need you to sign these."

Natalie's smile vanishes.

"What?" I say, flummoxed. "Why?"

"Limited edition, innit," explains Tanya. "I'm getting all the artists to sign the first ten copies – makes people want them more. More desirable and that."

(Ha! How exciting! I'm an *artist* that needs to *sign* something…) I mean, Tanya does have a flair for this business malarkey; if she thinks me signing something will make it better, who am I to argue?

I glance at Nat. She doesn't look as impressed by how great this is as I'd hoped she would.

"Oh right," I say, trying to look contrite.

"Come on, *chop chop*," barks Tanya. I sit at my desk and start signing the comics.

"Nat, this won't take a sec," I say, aware I probably sound way too happy about it. "And then we can talk about what we're going to do later on the project."

"Hey, Jessica," says Hannah, coming over. "Maybe I should get you to sign the rabbit picture you drew for me as well?"

"No, no, no," interjects Tanya. "No freebies. My girl does this for money now."

Hannah looks a bit scared.

"Ha ha! Only joking," adds Tanya. "Twenty pence. No, I'm joking again. She's free till she's famous."

65

"Great." Hannah smiles, slightly confused but relieved, and passes me her rough book. I grin bashfully. This is *unreal*. It's not just Tanya's publicity stunt – someone actually *wants* my autograph!

"Uh, do you want me to write anything in particular?" I try to sound casual. This is so exciting! (Am I milking it?)

"Um." Hannah pauses in thought. "Put 'To Hannah' and then sign your name."

"Classic choice," I hear myself say. *Classic choice?* Where am I getting this from? And how would I know what counts as a *classic choice* in the world of autographing? It's the first time this has ever happened.

I write as neatly as I can. I want Hannah to be glad I'm signing her rough book. Then I pass it back to her. "How's that?"

Jessica X

"Great!" Hannah bcams. "Thanks!"

Hurray! I'm awesome. I grin bashfully. I feel like I might not ever be able to stop grinning. I try to make a joke, so I put on a posh accent and say, "Any time, *daaahling*!" And I wave my hand pretentiously, like I'm some kind of fabulous actress type. Hannah chuckles and walks back over to her desk.

I look back towards Nat, who is now staring at me slightly incredulously, like she can't quite believe what she's seeing.

"Hey, um, nearly done," I say, managing to hold eye contact, but only just.

"Nat, babes, it looks like Jessica might be a while. Do you want to come over to *my* desk and we can go through the stuff we still need for my sleepover on Saturday?" says Amelia.

"Yes," says Nat.

"Great. It's going to be brilliant. I *so* can't wait for you to meet Scarlett," trills Amelia as they march off. *Urrgh* Scarlett. *Urrrgh* Amelia, come to that.

I scribble my name over the remaining comics as quickly as I can. Does Nat want me to feel *guilty* or something? I haven't done anything wrong. It's not *my* fault I have to sign autographs now.

I'm really glad that people like my cartoons. This is the first time in my life I've been good at something that other people vaguely care about. I should be allowed to enjoy it without Nat getting all huffy.

I finish signing the comics and try to explain this to Nat before the bell goes. "Hey, Nat, don't be annoyed with me," I say.

"I'm not annoyed," she replies unconvincingly.

"It's just," I falter, "you know … this is what my public expects of me."

"*What your public expects of you?*" Natalie's eyes bulge kind of wide. "Have you *heard* yourself lately?"

"Look—" I try and explain.

"You know you don't *have* a public, right?" says Nat. "You're in Year Six. You're *eleven*."

"Look, we're getting off track. I didn't say I could even *do* the wildlife project this lunchtime. You can't be annoyed with me for that. I'm really busy, so if you want to hang out with me we have to make plans."

"Oh, *really*?" Nat folds her arms. "Well, we didn't used to." I'm pretty sure we *did* used to. But I'm not

68

getting anywhere with this argument, so I give up.

Maybe Nat's actually jealous that I'm famous now. Maybe this is really hard for her. Maybe she *preferred* it last term when I was doing all the running.

Obviously I have totally forgiven Natalie for the way she behaved to me last term. *Obviously*. But there is maybe the teeniest, tiniest part of me that feels *pleased* that, hey, sometimes I'm just too busy signing autographs to hang out with her.

I feel slightly tense as I trudge into double maths though – and not just because I think maths was invented as a practical joke to torture schoolchildren. I mean, partly that, obviously. But I don't really like it when Natalie's annoyed with me. Luckily she seems fine again at break time.

$\sqrt{26} =$

Then it's double art, which is a lot more enjoyable. And not just because it's my favourite lesson of all time, or because I always have loads of fun sitting with Megan, Emily, Fatimah, Joshua and (even) Terry. But because the comic is proving to be a *hit*! I *knew* it would be!

This is so great.

"I *love* the sheep on the front," says Emily, giggling.

"That's *so* Miss Price," agrees Megan.

"It even looks like her," says Terry.

"I like the sheep," says Fatimah. "And Roland. Well, I like all of it. It's brilliant."

Then they keep reading out bits of our fake gossip on the back cover and giggling.

I'm slightly worried our art teacher, Mrs Cooper, might hear them laughing or see the comic (especially as Terry isn't exactly known for his subtlety) but somehow we get away with it. And we still manage to draw the seashells that Mrs Cooper has put in the middle of everyone's tables.

"Right," says Tanya at lunchtime. "First meeting since the launch. I think it went well and that. You?"

Joshua, Lewis and I nod our agreement on the comfy seats outside the library.

"The signed copies have gone like hot cakes," Tanya informs us. "Knew that would pay off.

I saw it on *Cash in the Attic*."

"Oh, clever," I say.

"Of course, they might also have gone like hot cakes because they're free," points out Lewis.

"That's next on the agenda, Lewis, me old mucker," says Tanya. "Shall we start charging? Say it was free to start with, then charge 20p for the next one?"

This causes much debate. So much in fact that we don't really discuss anything else about the next issue and by the end we still haven't resolved if we're charging or not. We do discuss our plans for world domination a bit (mainly build up an audience and portfolio here at school, then try and sell it in a comic shop and online, and then…

BOOM!

It goes viral).

But you know, we probably need to get a *few* more issues under our belts first. I mean, we're not *quite* ready for that yet. It's not like we're not *realistic*.

I don't get a chance to tell them about my awesome idea for the bee and the wasp having an argument.

The price is kind of irrelevant anyway, as far as I'm concerned. As I said before, the comic is being made on Lewis's dad's computer and printed on his fancy printer for free (well, unknown to him). So it's not as if we actually pay for production or anything.

"You all right?" asks Joshua as we pack up our stuff at the end of lunch and start heading back to our form rooms.

"Yeah, why?" I ask.

"You were a bit quiet in the meeting. You didn't keep chipping in and making us listen to your latest *brilliant* ideas for the comic, like you normally do."

He looks amused.

"Am I really annoying about the comic?" I ask then. I mean, Nat's been annoyed; Cherry and Shantair have previously been forced to actually tell me to shut up. Is there a pattern forming here?

"No, you're funny," says Joshua, looking slightly surprised.

So I explain to Joshua about how Nat got annoyed when I had to sign the comics this morning and I put on a posh accent, but I was joking. "And I *tried* to explain to her that it's what our public expect of us," I finish.

"Our … what now?"

"Public," I repeat.

"Um, I think I might have isolated the problem," says Joshua drily.

"All right, all right, so that might have made me sound big-headed." I start to see the funny side. Joshua is chuckling.

"Look, it's OK if you're a *bit* big-headed," he says. "Your cartoons are really good, and funny. But you know, don't get *carried away*."

"Good plan," I reply.

73

Natalie and I make some progress on our project at her house after school. It's good reading all the literature together because I think that actually I might have trouble understanding some of it on my own. But when there are two of us, we kind of keep each other going. And sometimes if I don't get something, Nat can explain it, and sometimes if Nat doesn't get something, I can explain it.

We don't finish reading *everything*. It's not the sort of thing you can just read overnight, no matter how keen Nat is to do this, and she makes me promise to have a look through the rest of it myself later on.

I get dropped off home by Lisa, Natalie's mum, and enter my kitchen to find Ryan and my parents in the middle of another argument about Kit Kats.

"Really, Ryan," says my dad, surprisingly crossly, "the Super Saver Value chocolate-covered wafer biscuits are practically the *same thing*. I don't understand what your problem is."

"But they're *not* the same!" insists Ryan.

"Hi, gang," I say. "I take it you all missed me loads."

"Yes, of course." My mum pats me affectionately on the head, though she looks tired.

74

"It's been terrible," says Ryan sombrely. I repress a smile at how serious he seems. I'm a pretty excellent big sister most of the time. So it's understandable that it would be terrible when I'm not here to make things awesome.

"But," says Ryan to Dad. "You said the economy drive was *over.*"

"It *is*, now we are *tightening our belts*," says my dad. "End of discussion."

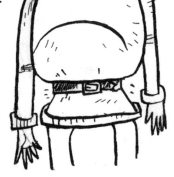

"Well, *tightening our belts* is really just a *euphemism* for economy drive though," I say helpfully.

I don't know why my dad isn't more aware of this. He's got into trouble with euphemisms before.

Once when my Auntie Joan (my mum's sister) came to stay my dad said to her, "You look really well, Joan!" And Joan got quite irate and said, "Oh, I look *well*, do I? Is that a euphemism for *fat*, Bert?" And my dad got quite flustered and said it wasn't.

"We have to cut back on certain things, Ryan," says my dad firmly. "That's just the way it is. As I said, end of discussion."

"But why can't we cut back on *other* things?" whines Ryan, not picking up on the *end of discussion* vibe my dad is trying to give out.

"Like what?" I ask him curiously.

"Toothpaste," supplies Ryan, and I chuckle.

"Toothpaste is an essential, Ryan. We're not cutting back on essentials to make room for luxuries," snaps my dad. "*End of discussion.*"

"Nice try though," I tell Ryan.

"Plus all your teeth would fall out of your head and then you wouldn't be able to eat Kit Kats anyway," says my mum.

The doorbell rings. My parents look at each other in confusion. "Who could that be at this hour?" asks my dad.

"Jessica is here. Tammy has a key," says my mum. "Unless, could she have lost it?"

My dad goes to the front door, and we all follow him suspiciously down the corridor, trying to peer over his shoulder. It occurs to me that this is one time we might wish we had Ryan's rounders bat to hand.

My dad opens the door and we hear an excitable shriek. "*Surprise!*" It's Auntie Joan!

Chapter 8

Auntie Joan is awesome. She isn't afraid of anyone. I think she might have started more fights with strangers than my mum and Tammy put together. But somehow she manages to combine it with still being super fun and entertaining. She's the only person I've ever seen make my mum really laugh.

"Joan! Come in, what on earth—" begins my mum.

"I thought I'd surprise you!" My aunt bustles past my dad into our hallway and hugs my mum, then me, then Ryan.

My dad closes the front door. "Great to see you, Joan!" he says, trying to sound more enthused than he looks. Then, perhaps trying to make up for last time and distance himself from his faux pas, he suddenly adds, "You look really thin!"

Joan breaks off her hug with Ryan to glare at my dad. "*Thin*, Bert?" she responds. "Are you saying I look *ill*?"

"No, no, of course not," stammers my dad, looking flummoxed. Poor dad. He can't win, really.

My mum shoots my dad an apologetic look, but still says, "*Really*, Bert."

"I'll put the kettle on!" My dad takes himself out of the firing line and into the kitchen.

My mum once told me that when Joan and my dad first met they didn't really like each other, but that they get on fine now. I think my mum might need to look up "fine" in the dictionary.

The best things about my aunt's visits are that she loves spending time with Ryan and me, and taking us to fun places. The downside is that sometimes some of the places are "educational". And sometimes if she thinks we're watching too much television, she goes on about it turning us into "damn idiots". But, you know, you can't have everything.

My aunt works in the music industry. Which I thought was really cool when I first heard about it – I thought maybe she could introduce me to popstars and I could make everyone at school jealous – but it turns out she works with orchestras and stuff. The reason she's in town is because she's "on tour" with one of them.

And no one's impressed by orchestras. Well, actually Cherry is. She's got Grade Three on the clarinet, though, so that doesn't make it something I could really boast about *in general*.

My Auntie Joan is filling us in on how great her hotel is when my dad comes back in with a tray of tea and some Super Saver Value digestive biscuits.

"Don't push the boat out on my account," says Joan, eyeing the biscuits with disdain as if Dad has deliberately insulted her again.

"It's all we have in," explains my mum.

"We're on an economy drive," I elaborate.

"No, we are *tightening our belts*," says my dad obstinately.

"Potato *potarto*," I quip, and my aunt chuckles.

"Do you have any Kit Kats on you?" Ryan asks Joan.

"No, little monkey, but I tell you what I *do* have." Joan leans towards Ryan. "I've got your nose!" She takes a pretend swipe at his nose and puts her thumb between her fingers.

Ryan giggles as she tickles him but then sighs patiently. "I know you haven't," he says firmly, as if fending off a conman.

Joan takes a teacup from my dad, places it on her lap and then wipes the spoon on her T-shirt, as if she didn't think my dad would have given her a clean enough spoon. Then she stirs her tea. My parents exchange a look but don't say anything.

"Well, maybe I can take the kids out and pick up a few things? Kit Kats, and whatnot?" says Auntie Joan.

"Yeeeeaaaaahhhh!" Ryan sinks on to the floor and hugs Joan's knees. She pats his head affectionately.

"No," says my dad a bit too quickly, sitting down once the tea and biscuits are distributed. "We think it's good that the children learn a bit about fiscal responsibility, and that they can't always have what they want."

"Oh," says Joan, unimpressed. "Well, that's no fun."

"Exactly," I say.

"Well, I'm taking you all out for dinner some time," proclaims Joan. "You let me know when suits. I'm down for a bit."

"Thank you," says my mum, glancing at my dad. "That would be lovely, Joan."

"I don't get *anything* I want," Ryan mumbles.

"Oh, I see," says Joan teasingly. "And you think Jessica does, do you?"

Ryan starts giggling. "Yes!"

"Want all the latest fashions, do you?" She addresses me.

"If by fashions you mean felt tips, then yes," I reply.

"Well, just you remember," says Joan, "the prettiest thing you can wear is a smile."

"What if you have no teeth?" asks Ryan.

(This is one of the things I love about having a six-year-old around. They ask the questions no one else will.)

Joan pauses, unsure what to say, then goes for, "Even then."

She continues sympathetically. "It can be tough when money's tight. Janet, do you remember when we were teenagers and I used to go busking for extra cash? Gawd, those were the days!"

"What did you play?" I ask.

"Violin or guitar mostly," says my aunt. *Hmmm*, I think, *so there's actually a practical application to learning an instrument?*

"Did it work?" asks Ryan.

"Oh yeah!" enthuses my aunt. "In the summer I could rake it in."

"But times are very different now," says my dad quickly. "It would be far too dangerous to try something like that these days." He raises his eyebrows at Auntie Joan.

"What? Oh, yes. Sure. Dangerous," says Auntie Joan.

Then Joan tells us about some of the crazy things that happened on her journey here. Which mainly seem to involve her shouting at a man on the train who dropped a crisp packet on the floor, possibly accidentally – we don't know. But then Auntie Joan said to him, "I didn't realise your mum worked here."

He looked at her, slightly confused, and said, "Sorry?" so Joan had repeated her sentence.

Then, when the man confirmed his mum didn't work on the train, Joan went in for the kill and said, "Oh well then, I guess you'd better pick up your litter YOURSELF!" *Pow*, just like that.

As much as I'm glad I wasn't there *with* her (that would have been really embarrassing) it does sound quite funny. Though I feel a bit sorry for the man, who obviously didn't know what to do with my aunt. She can be very cutting and sarcastic to people she doesn't like. Although clearly that man deserved it, because as my aunt said, he brought it on himself by being a "damn idiot".

"You see, kids? It's important to stand up to bullies." Joan is addressing Ryan and me. (Bully? *Really?* A man dropping a crisp packet?) "If you believe in something, you have to fight for it. All that it takes for evil to prevail is for good men – or women – to do nothing. It's a famous quote. I forget who said it."

"Edmund Burke," supplies my dad, and everyone looks at him, impressed – even Joan. "He was a politician in the 1700s." Sure, we sometimes *mock* my dad for enjoying bird programmes and reading history books for fun, but every now and then he proves it all has a point.

"Well, there we go," concludes my aunt.

Chapter 8

"Hi, babes! Come in!" Amelia opens her front door and ushers Nat and me inside. "Scarlett's not here yet."

It's Saturday night and something suddenly dawns on me about Amelia's sleepover as I step into her house. I'm about to spend upwards of sixteen hours with the squealy, snooty CAC girls who essentially bullied me last term.

Hmmm. I might not have thought this through. On the plus side, there *will* be fizzy wands. Natalie and Amelia's organisational skills have made sure of that.

"Oh my God, so it's just my cousin Scarlett to arrive now," says Amelia excitedly, as we all sit cross-legged in a circle in her living room, surrounded by sleeping bags and sweets. "She's just amazing! I can't wait for you all to meet her. We're like sisters!"

"Oh *God*, you mean there's *two* of you?" I blurt out. Everyone sort of stops smiling and looks at me. "Joking, joking," I quickly add, waving my hand for Amelia to continue talking.

"Actually," says Amelia, returning warmly to her subject, "like, we totally used to be the same at everything. We were born a month apart—"

"Wow!" interrupts Cassy.

"I know," agrees Amelia. "And our mums used to say we were like sisters and stuff. But now we're older we're, like, cool in different ways. Like, I'm really cool and into high fashion and stuff, and Scarlett is, like, really alternative."

"Like how?" asks someone called Naomi.

"Loads of ways, like, oh my God, she dyed her hair bright red when she was, like, ten!"

"She *dyed* her hair?" gasps Cassy.

"Yes. Her mum was going to *kill* her, but, like, she'd totally already done it, so there was nothing she could do."

"That's so cool. She sounds amazing," says Naomi.

The doorbell rings. Amelia squeals and jumps up,

returning shortly with Scarlett.

Scarlett has a cool red bobbed haircut, cropped leather jacket, henna tattoos on her hands and is wearing a lot of bracelets.

"Oh. Em. *Gee*. It's so good to see you, Ames," Scarlett says to Amelia, as Amelia introduces her to everyone.

Wait. Did Scarlett just say *oh em gee* instead of *oh my God*? Is she trying to save time, like in a text? But they both have the *same number* of syllables. I smirk at Natalie but she doesn't notice.

OH EM GEE

There's a moment's silence before Cassy breaks the ice by saying, "Cool bag," to Scarlett.

"Thanks! I got it from Camden Market. It's, like, totally from the seventies or something."

Everyone agrees that's really cool. I start to wonder if I'm the only person who doesn't have an in-built cool-o-meter.

Scarlett happily answers more questions about her clothes.

"And this belt is actually *Prada*." (There's an audible gasp from Amelia.) "It belonged to my mum, so it's like totally vintage."

"Wow, *vintage*," murmurs Naomi. And before I know it, everyone starts describing their outfit selections to Scarlett and Amelia. Scarlett generously praises everyone's choices. She calls their clothes "pieces".

I have to try not to laugh. I just can't take all this talk of fashion statements seriously. Everyone's acting as if we're at the Oscars or something.

Then I figure, if you can't beat them, join them. So I say to Natalie, "Darling! You look fabulous! And *who* are you wearing?" in my comedy-posh voice.

Natalie giggles and jokily poses, pretending to be a model. "My T-shirt was made by the Hello Kitty

people for me, especially for tonight."

"I, myself, am sporting the latest range from Tesco, and I think it really is this season's must-have outfit," I reply. Nat and I laugh.

Scarlett breaks off from showing the others all her bracelets to glare at me. "Actually," she says icily, "if there's one outfit in this room that I *don't* like, it's probably Jessica's. It's just not cool and it doesn't suit you at all," she adds loftily.

Wow, *burn*. I have been attacked by the fashion police. I don't care though, because I am a *cartoonist*, and I am above such trivial matters.

"Hey, sorry," I say. "I was just joking, I didn't mean to offend you." I take the high road.

"Well, I *did* mean to offend you," replies Scarlett.

Yikes, *strike two*! This girl really doesn't like me! I start to feel a bit hot. I don't care what Scarlett thinks, but I don't want to start getting bullied again or end up in a verbal fight at a sleepover.

"Yeah, we were just joking," Natalie adds, trying to smooth things over. "We thought you'd laugh."

"Oh, that's OK," says Scarlett sweetly to Nat. "I really like *your* outfit. The T-shirt is a nice piece. It's just Jessica who looks terrible."

"*Anyway*," interrupts Amelia, quickly changing the subject to save her party. "Let's choose what pizzas to order!"

"Oh, babes, before I forget, I'm totally vegetarian

now," says Scarlett. "So I can't have any meat pizzas."

"Wow, vegetarian," murmurs Cassy.

"No problem," says Amelia. "We'll order loads, so you can have the veggie ones."

Things do calm down then, which is a relief. I whisper to Nat that Scarlett seems a bit mean, but Nat seems to still think she's OK, just a bit sensitive.

After we've eaten take-away pizza (awesome) and played the memory game for sweets (I win some Percy Pigs – thank you, thank you very much), we get changed into our pyjamas to watch the first film.

I sometimes wish Nat could see things the way I do more. If someone had insulted *her* but been nice to me, I'm sure I'd still take Nat's side. I mean, Tanya Harris *did* do that last term, and I defended Nat. Initially. Before Nat stopped speaking to me.

90

Oh well, *I* know I'm awesome, and that's all that matters. I love how being good at cartoons protects me from how insecure I used to feel all the time. *In your face, snooty overdressed lady*, I think silently at Scarlett. *I am a* cartoonist. *I operate outside your ideas of good and bad. I don't need your approval.* Ha.

"Hey, what's that?" Cassy is looking at something on a pad by Scarlett's bag. "It's really good. Did you do that?"

"Oh, yeah," replies Scarlett, casually picking up the pad. "I'm really good at cartoons. I'm going to be a cartoonist when I grow up."

OK, um. *What?*

Chapter 10

No, seriously. What the *what*?

"Wow, what else can you draw?" asks Naomi. Everyone starts crowding around Scarlett.

"Oh, loads of stuff. This is one of my originals," she says, sketching something else out on the pad.

"Check this out, Natalie, it's brilliant," says Cassy. Nat and I troop over to see the pad. Scarlett is drawing a sort of gangster mouse-type thing. (It's OK, I suppose.)

"That's great," says Nat.

"I told you Scarlett was amazing," says Amelia proudly.

"I've never really liked cartoons before, but you make them seem so cool," says Cassy.

Well, I suppose I shouldn't have expected my *Hell*fern comic to have reached the snooty CAC half of GUF, but *still*. I feel surprisingly stung by Cassy's pronouncement. My cartoons are *cool*, thank you very much. (Even if I, myself, am not.)

"Hey, Jess is really good at cartoons too," says Nat then.

"Oh, *really*?" Scarlett looks up at me.

"Yes," answers Nat. "She drew a brilliant dolphin on the front of my rough book for me, and her Mickey Mouse looks just like the real thing."

"Oh, right," says Scarlett. "Well, I try to make sure I draw my own *original* ones," she adds dismissively. "Anyone can copy stuff."

Wow. Well, firstly, not *everyone* can copy stuff to my level of accuracy. Otherwise it wouldn't be impressive. And secondly, what's her problem? Everyone *loves* her cartoons. *I'm* the one that should feel annoyed here. It's bad enough she's stolen the one thing I'm actually good at; she doesn't have to act all huffy about it.

"I do my own *originals* too," I say flatly, starting to feel annoyed.

"Oh really, like what?" Scarlett addresses me again.

"Well, um, bees, sheep, all sorts," I reply. Probably didn't big that up enough.

ONLY IF YOU SAY IT IN FRENCH!

"Right, yeah, doesn't sound very good. And I have more than just *two*."

"Well, it *is* very good, *actually*," I hear myself say.

"And they're in a comic that I co-invented."

So *ha*! Take that! (I really shouldn't be rising to this.)

"Oh right. You like comic books?" I have Scarlett's full attention now. "And what comics do you like?" She looks at me quizzically.

Damn. I don't actually know anything about proper comics. I just like cartoons. Scarlett is trying to *pull rank* on the cartoons front. And she's going to *win*.

"*Hang on,*" pipes up a voice in my head. "*Win what? What is this? Don't let this turn into a competition,*" the reasonable voice continues. "*Just step away.*"

But then I look at Scarlett, staring at me with a kind of scathing disdain, and this other voice goes, "*Shut up, reason! We're taking her* down*!*"

But then the reasonable voice points out that I don't have to pretend to be something I'm not. And I realise that's true, so I just say, "Well, I don't really like comic books as such. I just sort of like *The Simpsons* and *Futurama*. I'm a big fan of Gary Larson's *Far Side* stuff. And I have Matt Groening's *Huge Book Of Hell*."

"Oh right. I thought you would be into comics. Oh well. *I* really like Spiderman."

"Great," I say, unsure what to do with this information. *I don't care, I don't care. I'm still a great cartoonist. Hakuna Matata*, I say to myself. "My friend Joshua likes Spiderman," I add.

"Oh, right, cool," says Scarlett, as if drawing a line under the conversation.

"Hey, draw something else," Cassy asks her.

"Sure thing," says Scarlett, and she sketches a few more pictures, to general oohs and aahs from her captive audience. No one asks me to draw anything.

"I get loads of my inspiration from the underground scene," says Scarlett.

And what exactly is the underground scene? I wonder. I'm guessing she doesn't mean the tube map. But no one asks her a question that pushes that issue.

Honestly, I think as we're getting into our sleeping bags later on. First Amelia moves here and steals my best friend, and *now* her stupid cousin comes along and steals my whole identity. They might actually be the worst family in the world.

I feel less aggrieved in the morning. I'm quite impressed with the power of sleep. I realise I still have everything I want. I have Natalie back, we're doing the wildlife project together and I have my very own comic with its own audience. I don't need the CAC half of GUF to like me as well. Scarlett can't hurt me. I'll probably never see her again.

I'm supposed to be spending all of Sunday with Natalie, so I'm slightly disappointed when Amelia succeeds in convincing Nat to accompany her and Scarlett to the mall to show Scarlett all our town's shops. This effectively means I'm trapped into spending more time with Scarlett, but at least I feel more able to rise above any jealousy now.

Trudging around a mall with people I don't really like as they witter on about what looks good and what looks, like, lame, is not my cup of tea, but I manage to zone out and think about what cartoons I would like to draw next for the comic.

"They have some really lovely stuff in here, Jess." Natalie's voice snaps me back to attention in the accessories shop. Everyone is looking at bracelets, necklaces and hats.

"*Love* this," says Scarlett, trying on a funky, knitted hat. "This would go really well with my vintage Gucci belt." She gestures at her waist.

"I thought you said your belt was Prada?" I say, confused.

"Did I?" says Scarlett absently.

"Yeah, last night you said it was vintage Prada because it was your mum's," I confirm.

"Oh, I think I must have meant another belt," says Scarlett, unfazed, and she tries on another hat.

But something strikes me as odd about that. If you were so pleased with your amazing designer belt, surely you wouldn't just *forget* which *brand* of amazing designer-ness it was? I mean, surely that's the whole *point* of spending insane money on an everyday item? It makes it *special* so you remember? It starts to make me think they're not even designer at all. There's something odd about Scarlett. (And she *says* OMG.)

Nat puts a silver necklace with a star pendant round my neck. "This looks good on you, Jess," she says.

"I don't need it," I reply, glancing in the mirror. "I've already got the best friends necklace you gave me. I don't need two necklaces."

"Oh, I have *loads* of necklaces," responds Scarlett.

"You can never have too many," agrees Amelia.

"You can have *two* necklaces," says Nat. "Besides, it's really pretty on you."

"The prettiest thing you can wear is a smile," I reply sagely, quoting my Auntie Joan.

Nat laughs. "The prettiest thing you can wear is a smile *and this necklace*," she counters. "You should totally buy it."

I don't have any money. There is no way I'm buying the necklace even if I am starting to slightly like it a bit. "Thanks, Nat, but I might think about it and come back if I still like it later," I say and take it off, knowing full well I am never going to come back for it. My family are *tightening our belts* and I have to be immune to consumerism. Kind of.

As we leave the shop (after the others have all bought some hair clips and bracelets) I hear someone shouting my nickname.

"Oi-oi! It's Toons!" I look round and see Michael, Joshua's friend, with Joshua and some of the rest of the basketball team, loitering by a bench. *Hey*, what are they doing here? I grin.

I still never know quite what to make of them. I

always used to feel nervous of larger groups of boys, in case they shouted "Ooh, chess club" or other names at me. But since meeting these basketball boys through Joshua, after Tanya circulated my cartoons, they've always been really nice to me. Part of me still sometimes feels a bit nervous, none the less.

"Do you know them?" whispers Scarlett.

"Yes, well, Jess does really," Nat whispers back.

I wave back at them and they come over to us. Michael hi-fives me, and then (as if he didn't mean to be quite this civil) he playfully shoves me away. I laugh and say, "Oi."

"Hello, hello," says Joshua, smiling.

"Hey, Joshua," I reply.

"Oh, so *this* is Josh," says Scarlett. *Joshua,* I think crossly. *Get his name right.*

"Who's your friend?" asks Michael. "And what happened to her hands?" He gestures to Scarlett's henna tattoos.

"Oi, love, you've got pen on you. Did you know?" says someone called Damon.

Some of the boys laugh.

"Sorry, ignore them," says Joshua. "Hi, I'm Joshua."

"Scarlett," says Scarlett, extending her hand and shaking his. "I've heard *so* much about you."

"Have you?" Joshua looks surprised and glances at me. *That is a lie*, I think, annoyed. She has heard *one* thing about him.

"Yes. You like Spiderman, don't you?" continues Scarlett. And *that* is the one thing, there.

"Yeah!" says Joshua, looking slightly relieved. "I love Spiderman."

"Me too," says Scarlett, giving Joshua what I might have to describe as a winning smile.

"Really?" he says. "Peter Parker or Miles Morales?"

"Oh, I like both, Josh," says Scarlett.

"Blimey, a girl who knows about Spiderman," says Joshua, sounding annoyingly impressed.

His name is not Josh, it's Joshua! I want to shout. Where are the Ting Tings when you need them? *That's not his name!* Scarlett can't give Joshua a nickname before I do. She's only just *met* him.

"So what are you gents up to?" Scarlett just starts

effortlessly chatting away to the boys, and soon Michael and Damon seem to have forgotten they found her hands so amusing, and are engrossed in conversation. Considering Scarlett is only eleven like us, she's very confident.

Joshua and I catch up about our weekends. It's quite fun to hear about his basketball practice, and I tell him about my crazy auntie.

"Sounds like she'd make a good sheep character," he jokes.

"Yeah," I agree. Though truthfully, I'm not sure I'd *dare*. Just in case she ever found out. The wrath induced by a dropped crisp packet would be nothing compared to that.

"Oh, Jess, before I forget, do you want to come to this comic convention thing with me?" asks Joshua. "Lewis was going to come, but now he can't. It's next Saturday. Should be a laugh, and my dad will drive us."

I sneak a glance at Scarlett. I can't be sure but I might have seen a small flicker in her expression when Joshua mentioned the word comic. I don't know if she can hear us. I don't want her to hear us.

"Yeah, cool, why not?" I say, trying not to get distracted. "I mean, I'll have to check with my mum but I'm sure it will be fine." This could be *fun*.

"Great," Joshua smiles. Then he starts chatting about his new idea for the next Roland comic strip. It sounds brilliant, but I kind of don't want to talk about it too much in earshot of Scarlett.

At the moment Joshua doesn't know that Scarlett draws cartoons, and she doesn't know he's involved in the comic. And something is making me want to keep it that way.

"Sounds really funny," I say. "Let's talk about it on Monday."

"Yeah, definitely talk about it on Monday," agrees Joshua. "Have you had any more ideas for the comic?"

"What's all this about a comic?" asks Scarlett, ending her conversation and butting into ours.

Nooooo, I think helplessly as Joshua starts explaining. Scarlett declares herself very impressed, and predictably reveals that she also considers herself a cartoonist. *Nooooo! I'm* the cartoonist! I want to shout. *Shut up, Scarlett.* The position is *filled.*

Nooooooooo!

Joshua tells her about his Roland strip, and then starts describing how funny my Miss Price sheep cartoon was, till Scarlett says she doesn't "get it". So Joshua explains about Miss Price in French lessons, and then Scarlett says, "Oh, *right*," and sort of half-laughs. "Maybe you had to be there," she adds.

"Other people think it's funny," I hear myself blurt out.

"Oh, I'm sure they do," says Scarlett, giving me a smile that I know is just for Joshua's benefit, so he won't see how vile she really is. "But, like, comedy is subjective, so don't feel bad if you can't please everyone. Like, I think Josh's Roland strip sounds really funny, but I think your sheep sounds a bit lame. Sorreee!"

WHAT? I'm momentarily blinded by rage, but I hold it together. "Uh, well, it made the *front cover*, so I think that speaks for itself," I retort pompously.

"*Riiight*." Scarlett acts nonplussed, then she turns brightly to Joshua again. "So, anyway, if you ever want something *fresh*, let me know." *Nooooooo.*

"Sure, sounds good," says Joshua. *Double noooooooo.*

"Here, I'll give you my card," says Scarlett,

handing Josh something. Scarlett has a *card*. Of course she does. *Infinity nooooooooo*. Get off my turf, you *witch*! I want to scream.

I'm just considering the various consequences of (a) starting to cry, (b) hitting Scarlett with a giant bat or (c) trying to create a distraction by shouting "Fire!" when Amelia unexpectedly comes to my aid.

"Scarlett, babes, have you seen the time?" she says. "We should probably get moving soon." Thank goodness Amelia still  finds comics boring. Though, really, the damage has already been done.

"Oh, yes, we should," agrees Scarlett. "And I want to pop into Boots before we head back. I can't be late for my dad or he'll go all Dr Jekyll on me and turn into an angry nutcase."

"Oh, actually Dr Jekyll was the nice one," I hear myself say.

"What?" says Scarlett. Everyone looks at me.

"Do you mean that book, *The Strange Case Of Dr Jekyll*

And Mr Hyde? Cos Dr Jekyll was the nice one. When he drank the potion he turned into Mr Hyde, who was the monster." I'm enjoying myself now and decide to elaborate. "I assume you were trying to liken your dad to a monster just then? Because, actually, you just called him an upstanding citizen."

Now who's the ignoramus? In your *face*, Scarlett! I raise one eyebrow, just to underline my victory. I know I'm being petty but hey…

Amelia looks as though she's wondering how on earth I knew that, but doesn't comment. To give credit where it's due, I picked it up on one of Auntie Joan's "educational trips". One of the last times she visited she insisted on dragging Ryan and me to the library to stave off "brain rot" on our way to becoming "damn idiots".

Ryan was allowed to choose a children's book but Joan insisted I pick mine from the "Classics" section as I was "getting older" now. I had protested but was ignored. In the end I chose *The Strange Case Of Dr Jekyll And Mr Hyde* because it looked the shortest. But I did end up reading it, and actually really enjoyed it.

"Well, anyway," says Scarlett dismissively, as if I have made some kind of weird faux pas rather than an insightful point. And we say goodbye to the boys and head off to Boots.

As we look at some bath products that smell like foods, my insides are doing cartwheels of anger and confusion. I try and enjoy sniffing the strawberry soap, coconut shampoo, cherry shower gel and chocolate bubble bath, but all I can think about is that I might have found someone I hate more than Amelia and Harriet VanDerk put together.

And then, as Amelia and Natalie marvel over how much the smell of the chocolate bubble bath is making them want a real chocolate bar, I see Scarlett slip one of the strawberry soaps into her bag. I'm too shocked to say anything.

"Time to go," she announces.

We all leave and go home.

Chapter 11

I *knew* there was something wrong with Scarlett. She's not just Amelia mark 2 with added drawing skills; she's actually a *criminal*. I have witnessed a *crime*. I could go on *Crimewatch*.

I am a witness! Like in that film *Witness*. Sure, it was just a tiny soap and the odds are I wouldn't get a new identity or go into witness protection because of it, but taking it was against the law and Scarlett is therefore a villainous delinquent.

I can't wait to tell everyone. Except … maybe the time to do that was at the mall? She could easily hide the evidence now. But then, is my *not* coming forward further perverting the course of justice? Or maybe I should keep it under my hat for now, but then if Scarlett gets any more annoying I can bust out what a petty thief she is?

What is that noise? I'm taken out of my reverie by some high-pitched notes. It sounds eerily like "Twinkle Twinkle Little Star", but played on a xylophone or something. Honestly, it's bad enough having Scarlett distracting me from working on the wildlife project without a strange noise coming from outside as well.

I go over to my window and look out. Ryan is sitting cross-legged in the middle of the front garden playing his xylophone (so it *is* indeed a xylophone). There's an upside-down cap in front of him. Oh my God, he's *busking*! He's busking in our front garden. He's even put some loose change in the hat.

"Thank you, thank you very much!" he calls out to no one in particular, finishing "Twinkle Twinkle Little Star". "Roll up! Roll up!" he shouts, and then launches into "Three Blind Mice". This is unbelievable. I can't help but admire him, though I'm pretty sure the repetitive nature of this high-pitched noise is going to get annoying pretty soon.

Sure enough, as I'm watching, a front door opens. "Hello there, young man," says Mr VanDerk. "What's all this noise you're making on a Sunday?" Typical VanDerk reaction; it's hardly loads of noise. And *their* kids are always practising piano that we can hear through the walls and *we* don't complain. To their faces.

"Hello!" says Ryan jovially. "I'm busking for money to buy Kit Kats. Would you like to pay me?"

"I'll pay you to stop!" says Mr VanDerk, and then chortles at his own joke.

I'm thinking of running downstairs to prevent Mr VanDerk doing irreparable damage to Ryan's self-esteem when *our* front door opens and my mum's voice joins the mix.

"What is going on here?"

"Hi, Mummy. I'm busking for money so we can afford to buy Kit Kats again," explains Ryan helpfully.

I can well imagine my mum's mortification at these words being spoken in front of a VanDerk. My parents like to pretend that everything is brilliant to the VanDerks, and this will have directly derailed their careful lies about how successful we are.

"Don't be silly, darling," says my mum. "Come inside, please."

But Mr VanDerk doesn't miss his opportunity to gloat. "Oh dear," he says. "They often overhear things they shouldn't, don't they?"

"But, Mummy, I'm busking!" Ryan sounds bewildered at being moved on.

"Inside *now*," says my mum tersely. Ryan huffily gets up and takes his things inside.

"Don't worry, I'm sure things will pick up," simpers Mr VanDerk.

"Well, I'd love to stay and chat but I must get back inside," my mum replies.

The front door closes but this is only the start of the incident.

"What do you *mean*, he was busking outside?" I hear my dad say. Then everything gets muffled. I go towards my door to hear better.

"But, Daddy, I *did* listen. It's not dangerous in the *front garden*," I hear Ryan explain.

"This is *your* doing, Joan!" my mum accuses my aunt.

"I don't see what the problem is," replies Joan.

"It's great he's trying to make something of himself. Better than watching TV."

"He's *not* trying to make something of himself!" My mum's voice is getting louder. "He's embarrassing our family in front of the neighbours. I don't want the whole street knowing our business!"

"There's nothing to be embarrassed about," retorts Joan, whose voice is also rising. "If your neighbours are *that* small-minded, that's *their* problem!"

"Joan, we have to live with these people!" replies my mum, sounding outraged.

"Calm down," says my dad, trying to soothe them both. "Let's keep our voices down. How about some tea? I'll put the kettle on."

My dad's noble attempt to mollify the situation seems, in fact, to be what finally ignites the fuse and sets off the explosion. Yikes.

If this was a cartoon, Ryan's busking would be a trail of gunpowder; my aunt and my mum reacting would be a cellar full of dynamite; and my dad telling them to calm down would be a lit match landing on the gunpowder which just so happens to lead to the cellar full of dynamite.

There is a tap at my door. I open it to find Ryan standing there looking confused and upset.

"Lego pirates?" I suggest, and he nods gratefully, disappearing into his room to retrieve his pirate ship and base camp.

I don't know when it started, but there's something weirdly comforting about playing Lego pirates with Ryan. It's like the outside world might change and be crazy, but there'll *always* be Lego pirates.

When I was feeling upset last term because of Natalie, it was really quite fun to just forget about all that and play a simple game of Lego pirates with Ryan. Plus it led to some ideas I wouldn't otherwise have had. The least I can do is return the favour when it's Ryan in the doghouse.

Ryan starts setting up the Lego on my carpet. I've said it before and I'll say it again: if my parents really wanted to save money, they should just go back in time and buy Ryan fewer toys. Admittedly, the outlay for inventing and developing a working time machine might well eat into any savings made by the endeavour, but *still*.

Ryan is quieter than usual and puts less gusto into explaining his new pirate storyline than he normally does. (The stripy-topped first mate is now called Clyde and he is missing in action after a storm. Turns out – sorry, spoiler alert – he's been kidnapped and is being held to ransom by another gang of pirates.) Even using the cannon doesn't make Ryan that happy. I decide to try and cheer him up.

"Don't worry, Ryan, they're all nuts," I say. Ryan giggles shyly, unsure. "This will soon blow over," I add. "I think Mum and Joan are genetically programmed to shout at each other or something. It isn't really even anything to do with you. It's just how they communicate."

Ryan nods, looking relieved, and lets fire another Lego cannon.

Chapter 12

Honestly, I think as I ride the bus to school on Monday morning, *my family is nuts*. Still, at least my mum apologised to Ryan for confusing and upsetting him. Even though her apology was slightly marred by Auntie Joan storming out of our house and refusing to be spoken to "like that" by my mum ever again. I'm pretty sure she'll be back though.

Anyway, at least everything is going really well with Natalie.

"What do you *mean*, you didn't read it?" explodes Natalie at registration when I reveal that I may not have actually *completely* finished reading the rest of the wildlife project literature. Eek. Well, things *were* going really well with Natalie.

"I've read *most* of it," I say, trying to backtrack. "Focus on the positives."

"Oh, *Jess*," sighs Natalie crossly. "Why didn't you finish it?"

I want to say: "Because there was a big fight at my house involving busking with a xylophone in the front garden, and I had to play Lego pirates with my little brother to cheer him up." But it sounds a bit … strange when you say it like that, so I don't.

"I'm really sorry, Nat. I didn't realise you were so keen to start everything right away," I say.

"Even though I *specifically* said I was?"

"Yeah, exactly. It was hard to know what you meant by that." I attempt humour.

A flicker of amusement crosses Natalie's face, but she manages to suppress it. "Jess, I'm serious about this."

"I know," I say contritely.

I really want to lighten the mood and make her laugh. I don't want her to be annoyed with me. I decide to go for broke. Go big or go home. I take a pretend swipe at Natalie's nose and put my thumb between my fingers. "I've got your nose!" I say in a silly voice.

116

Natalie looks like she is not going to crack but then she gives a massive grin and starts chuckling. "You are such a doofus!" she exclaims.

"That's why you love me," I reply.

"You promised you would work hard at this though."

"I know, and I will. I've said I'm sorry. Come on, I thought we were going to make it fun too."

"Yeah, we are." She smiles again and shakes her head at me.

Phew, the old got-your-nose trick might not work on Ryan but Natalie loved it. I probably can't *keep* doing it every time she's mad at me though. The novelty will wear off at some point.

I feel slightly frustrated as we file out to assembly. I don't want to have to keep appeasing Natalie like this. My life is exhausting enough. This was *meant* to be *fun*. I wish she'd chill out and enjoy it more.

There's nothing like a lovely Monday morning to make you glad you're alive. And this is *nothing* like a lovely Monday morning to make you glad you're alive. Ha ha, I am still funny though.

Luckily my morning lessons of double science and double PE pass by fairly uneventfully. It's fun to catch up with Cherry, Shantair, Megan, Emily and Fatimah. And even Tanya and Amelia seem in reasonably good spirits.

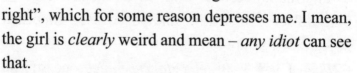

The only really bad thing that happens is a comment that Joshua makes at break time about Scarlett seeming "all right", which for some reason depresses me. I mean, the girl is *clearly* weird and mean – *any idiot* can see that.

"And she said OMG," I tell Cherry and Shantair at break, once Joshua is gone. "Like, oh em gee. Out loud, not in a text or anything. I mean, how ludicrous is that? You don't even save any time or anything!"

Cherry and Shantair exchange a slight look with each other, but then Shantair says, "That's true, it's the same number of syllables."

"*Exactly!*" I say. I *knew* my chess club friends would think Scarlett was an idiot. Why can't Joshua as well? Stupid Monday.

Instead of IT after lunch we're having another wildlife project lesson in the DT classroom. It turns out there's going to be a field trip soon, which does perk me up a bit.

The main upshot of this lesson is that we need to write to people who work with wildlife-type stuff to tell them we're doing a school project on their specialised subject and to ask them to send us information to help with our research. We get to practise our letter writing *and* pester semi-important people. What's not to like?

Well, I say *semi-important people*; one of the discussions this revelation immediately sparks is who to ask.

Mrs Cole has some strong ideas. In fact, she hands out a whole list of suggestions. Mostly various members of organisations for wildlife trusts, local councillors, charities and that sort of thing. They have been tipped off that we might be writing to them, and so are primed to respond quickly, leaving us with enough time to do the project.

But that is not how some people have chosen to

interpret this information. Natalie and I overhear lots of people blithely ignoring Mrs Cole's advice and saying they want to write to as many young celebrities and pop stars as they can crowbar into the project.

Everyone's favourite targets are the TV presenters who do a kids' wildlife show called *Cool For Cats*. (There's three of them, two girls, Melanie and Saz, and a boy, Martin, who some of the girls in our year fancy.) The *Cool For Cats* team also sometimes go on *Blue Peter* and show the presenters there how to hold a rabbit and stuff.

Mrs Cole can't help but hear this chatter as well and issues warnings several times. "Look, everyone, I know it's very tempting to write to more glamorous wildlife people, but think about how likely they are to reply. The *Cool For Cats* team probably gets loads of letters all the time, and just won't be able to reply to everyone, however much they may want to. I'd really prefer it if you stuck to the list."

No one appears to be listening. We can hear people

talking about asking them to come into school, and even helping them to do the final presentations to the rest of the class. Everyone's already got totally carried away from reality. To be completely honest, I can *sort of* see the appeal.

Nat takes the lid off her pen and marks something off the list. "Look," she says. "Everyone is going to pick really obvious TV people who won't ever write back. The *official* people will write back the quickest, so we'll get the work done quickly. So let's write to them."

"Yes," I say obediently. Though, actually, part of me had started thinking it might be fun to at least *try* and write to a celebrity. We don't *have* to always do everything exactly by the book. "Unless," I begin uncertainly, "are you sure that's not a little bit … boring?"

"*Jess!*" Natalie's face is like thunder. "Not you *as well*? Come *on*. We have to give ourselves the best possible chance of getting this done. No popstars are going to give a *monkey's* about a Year Six Wildlife Project, and you *know* that."

"Well, not the really famous ones, but you know, what if—"

"*No*." She interrupts me firmly. "The sooner we write to the boring official people, the sooner they will write back. And the sooner we can do the work."

"Yeah, I guess."

"And then there'll be more time left to draw *lots of pictures*," she adds with a shrewd smile.

Nat does know me pretty well. I feel a bit bad for thinking mean thoughts about her just now. I smile back apologetically.

"I do like to draw lots of pictures," I say. Nat giggles and calls me an idiot.

We pick two official wildlife experts and work well on our letters, finishing them by the end of the lesson. Now all I have to do is get a stamp from my parents when I get home, and post my letter. Then when we've got all the main work out of the way, nice and early, I'll be able to draw animals to my heart's content. Hurray.

I arrive home to find my dad watching TV on the sofa, looking slightly tired and a bit dejected.

"Hello, Jessica," he says, looking up as I come in. "Would you like to come and sit here with me? I'm watching Horace King's new bird programme. It's very interesting."

"Uh, sure." I drop my bag and slouch down next to him, though I doubt my dad and I have the same definition of the word *interesting*.

"I used to love Horace's kids' TV show when I was your age," says my dad. "I once made a bird feeder for the garden, just the way Horace showed us."

I briefly picture my dad's idyllic prehistoric childhood before being snapped back to the present when my mum bursts into the living room and says, "You'd better keep your son in here while I'm cooking. He's driving me *mad*!" Then she shoves a space-helmet-wearing Ryan through the door and disappears, slamming it behind her.

"I'm a SPACEMAN!" shouts Ryan, utterly unrepentant.

"*Shh*, Ryan, Dad's trying to watch a programme about birds," I say.

"I'M A SPACEMAN! I'M A SPACEMAN!" shouts Ryan. I *hate* it when he's like this. I feel annoyed I was so nice to him yesterday now.

"Shut up, Ryan!" I raise my voice. "We're watching TV here."

"Tape it, tape it, tape it," chants Ryan, spinning round loads, then falling over and making loud "death" noises.

"I can't tape it," says my dad sadly. "The thing's broken and we can't get a new one while we're tightening our belts."

"DADDY!" Ryan leaps up and into my dad's lap. "Let's play outside."

"Why doesn't Jessica take you outside and play?" says my dad hopefully.

"Sure," I say, starting to feel sorry for my dad.

"NO!" shouts Ryan, looking outraged. "*DADDY!*"

"KEEP IT DOWN IN THERE!" yells my mum from the kitchen.

"Come on then, Ryan." My dad sighs and stands up. "Let's go to the garden."

I think this is the first time I've felt sorry for one of my parents. I mean, I've *sympathised* with them loads in the past, *sure*. But ultimately I've generally thought it's their fault for *having* Ryan in the first place. Now I appreciate that they don't always get their own way either.

My poor dad. He's really quite a gentle and kind man, always making tea and trying to keep the peace. All he wants to do is watch one programme that his hero is in, and he can't even do that.

Then I have a brilliant idea.

Chapter 13

I'm still really excited about my brilliant idea on Saturday, when Joshua and his dad come to pick me up to go to the comic convention. (That's how brilliant an idea it is.) It's also a *secret* brilliant idea, and I never realised how exciting it can be, keeping secrets from people.

Nat and I have made pretty good inroads into the project this week too. We've been round each other's houses a couple of times, and I now know *loads* about insects, leaves and bee-keeping. Go ahead, ask me anything. I feel a bit bad I haven't even told Natalie my secret brilliant idea, but I think it's better this way. It will be more of a surprise.

Joshua's parents are divorced, and his dad is pretty much happy to take him wherever he wants on the weekends he stays with him. And he never says he's too busy as the whole point of the weekend is that he's not.

In some ways, that almost seems like a better arrangement than having two parents who are together but who collectively ignore you. I don't want my parents to get divorced or anything, but in some ways I envy Joshua's arrangement as a system. I can't remember the last time I spent a whole afternoon with one of my parents. My parents love it when we go out without them. My aunt is the one who takes us places.

Although in fact it turns out that Joshua's dad just sits in the café reading the paper while we go round the convention without him, which isn't as involved as I'd expected. But you know, whatever. The system still probably mainly works.

Joshua shows me some of his favourite comics and we have a smoothie each and talk about the different ways of drawing and what the best stories are. Then we join a queue to get an autograph of one of Joshua's favourite comic writers. I'm really enjoying myself. This is *fun*.

"Oh em gee! Josh, right?" Suddenly, from nowhere, Scarlett taps Joshua on the shoulder. *Nooooooooo!*

You know what's great about bumping into Scarlett? Absolutely nothing.

"Oh hi," says Joshua.

"Fancy meeting you here, Josh," she continues. Josh*ua,* I manage not to shout. There's a slight pause.

"You remember Jess too?" prompts Joshua. Scarlett seems keen to ignore me. But really, the feeling is mutual.

"Oh! Um, yes…" Scarlett pretends to rack her brains. "*Jen,* wasn't it?"

"Jessica," I say.

"Right, right, nice to meet you – sorry – see you again!" She laughs at her apparent confusion. "We met at the sleepover, didn't we?" I nod. Then (dropping all pretence at being nice) Scarlett adds icily, but quietly so Joshua doesn't hear, "I guess you're just quite *forgettable.*"

Honestly. We spent over sixteen hours together at that stupid sleepover and traipsing round that stupid mall. It was horrific. She spent *five minutes* chatting

128

to Joshua. It's such a pathetically obvious attempt to diss me, I feel sure Joshua will laugh at how transparent she's being, but he doesn't seem to have noticed how fake she is.

"Sorry, what did you say? I didn't catch it," I pretend. *Yeah, repeat it louder so Joshua can hear you insult me, you big faker*, I think.

"What?" says Scarlett. "Oh, by the way, I love what you've done with your hair," she says sweetly to me. "Really cool how you've made it look so messy, like you only just got up."

How *dare* – so rude! *Honestly*.

"I'm lucky, it just goes like this," I reply drily. Not going to give you the satisfaction of a reaction.

Unbelievably, *this* insult goes undetected by Joshua as well, just because it had the rhythm of a compliment.

"Can I cut in with you guys? The queue is, like, really long now."

"*No*," I hear myself say, before Joshua can answer. Scarlett and Joshua look at me. Well, Joshua looks; Scarlett kind of glares. "What?" I say, trying to sound reasonable. "I get really annoyed when people cut in in front of me. It's not fair."

"Oh, OK." Scarlett sounds dejected. "That's cool. It's just … I really love this guy and I'm worried I'll have to go home before I get to the front of the queue otherwise." She starts turning to leave.

"Hey, wait," says Joshua. She stops moving. (Is it me, or did she only move really slowly anyway? Like she *knew* this would work?) He turns to me. "She can cut in this once, can't she? If it means she doesn't miss out?"

"Oh, yeah. Sure!" I try to sound enthusiastic and upbeat rather than really annoyed. *Checkmate*. I can't really argue now. Well, I *can*, but not if I want to maintain the dignified moral high ground. I'm trapped by my stupid manners again.

Scarlett wastes no time and jubilantly starts jabbering away to Joshua like they're old friends. She keeps talking about things I've never heard of so I am really left out. Evil, horrible Scarlett. Joshua asked *me* to come here. If he wanted to see her all day he would have asked *her*.

We eventually make it to the front of the queue and Joshua and Scarlett get the comic writer's autograph. Joshua seems really dazed and starstruck afterwards.

"That was cool," he keeps murmuring.

"Are you guys hungry?" asks Scarlett. "I might just grab some food before I have to go home." *Oh, you suddenly have time for food?* I think cynically. *Thought you had to rush off? It's almost like you're a big liar.*

"I don't have any money," I reply flatly.

"Oh well, come with me anyway," she says, forcefully enough that the dazed Joshua starts following her, so I drag myself along too. Honestly, this is the *living end*.

To my slight surprise, Scarlett buys a hotdog. "I thought you were vegetarian?" I remark.

"What?" asks Scarlett, having swallowed her first bite. Joshua buys onion rings and offers me one.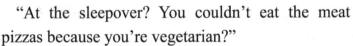

"At the sleepover? You couldn't eat the meat pizzas because you're vegetarian?"

"Oh right!" says Scarlett, as if she had completely forgotten about this. "Oh yeah, well, I *was* vegetarian then but, like, I kept fainting, so my doctor said I had to eat meat again."

"*Right*, right," I say, pretending to mull this over.

Something has clicked into place and Scarlett is now *officially* in the category of LIAR in my head. It's the only explanation. An attention-seeking liar. Possibly with pants on fire. She might even be a sociopath. (Plus she steals and says OMG out loud.)

"How's your comic going?" she asks. This nearly jolts Joshua out of his post-autograph buzz, but he still doesn't really seem to be listening. "Have you come up with any *good* ideas yet?" (She addresses this question to me.)

"Yeah, loads, thanks," I say crossly.

I finally got a chance to show the others my bee and wasp cartoon in our lunchtime meetings this week and they loved it. They want it to be the front cover. (I'd joked at the time that instead of Toons my new nickname should be Frontcover-o, but I don't think they got it. No one laughed and Joshua just kind of shook his head at me.)

But they must have really liked the bee cartoon because Joshua (finally alert and *back in the room*)

starts describing it to Scarlett now, and she actually laughs.

"You *like* my bee cartoon?" I blurt out, surprised.

"*Your* cartoon?" Scarlett sounds confused. "I thought Josh drew it?" Josh*UA*.

Ha ha! Busted! You only say you like things if you think Joshua did them, and hate things if you think I did them! Ha ha! Busted! A voice in my head starts gloating at Scarlett.

"No, I never said who drew it," says Joshua mildly, "just that it's probably going to be the front cover on the next issue, because it's the best out of all our ideas."

You hear that, Scarlett? The best *of all our ideas.* Quote unquote. *In your face!*

"So whoever has the best idea gets to be on the front cover?" says Scarlett.

"Yeah, obviously," says Joshua.

Obviously, Scarlett. I'm obviously the best. Get over it, I add in my head.

"Well, I should totally email you some of my cartoons and see what you think of them," concludes Scarlett.

Ha – wait, what? Noooo! Enough already. Let's

just leave it with me being the best.

"Great," says Joshua.

"*No!*" I accidentally shout, and they look at me oddly. "Er, what I mean is, you know, there's a commitee to sort of get through first; it has to be unanimous and everything. It's not fair on everyone else otherwise."

"That's true," says Joshua, "but if you email them to me, I can print them out and show them to the others and then we can all decide together."

"Oh right, yeah. *That's* a good idea." Now I'm the one who's lying.

"What's the matter?" asks Scarlett smugly. "*Scared* of a little competition?"

"Well, if I see some, I'll let you know," I reply just as smugly.

SNAP! Take that. *You evil-cartoonist-identity-copying-witch!* For the first time, Joshua seems to pick up on the fact that there is some tension between us. He looks quizzically from me to Scarlett.

"Oh, Josh," says Scarlett. "I, like, totally know the guy that runs your town's comic shop."

"You know Big Dave?" asks Joshua, surprised.

"Well, I don't know his name," concedes Scarlett,

"but he's friends with my cousin. Do you want me to see if he'll sell your comic there?" *What?*

"Wow!" Joshua nearly drops his onion rings, but luckily I grab them in time. "That would be amazing! Are you … sure?"

Oh, *as if* she knows him or has the power to make that happen.

"Yeah!" enthuses Scarlett. "Well, I'd have to ask him. But I'm sure he'd say yes."

"That would be … amazing!" Joshua is nearly lost for words he's so elated.

Once we've finally said goodbye to Scarlett, all Joshua can talk about is how cool it would be to sell our comic in a real comic shop. He's completely oblivious to how Scarlett is *obviously* just trying to bribe her way into our comic with more lies.

But when I politely hint that this is probably the case, he just tells me that my attitude towards the comic is "unhealthy" – which I think is pretty rich coming from the boy who just bought deep-fried onion rings.

Forget what I said before, *this* is the *living end*.

Chapter 14

My mum calls up the stairs as my dad answers the front door. "Kids! Best behaviour, please!" This is the first time my Auntie Joan has come round to our house since she and my mum had that big fight and she stormed out. I told you she'd be back.

"Joan!" enthuses my dad. "Great to see you! You look exactly the right weight for your height. You look beautiful and healthy and like you definitely have an appropriate BMI."

"Thanks," says Joan sceptically.

They've got this whole Sunday dinner planned. Roast chicken. Even Tammy is here (admittedly, partly to use the washing machine). It's actually my favourite of all the super-saver meals though. Cheap vegetables and roast stuff  tastes the same as normal-price vegetables and roast stuff. I don't see why we can't have this for every meal.

"Joan!" I hear Tammy yell from downstairs. "You'll sign my petition, won't you?"

"Of course I will," replies my aunt. "What's it for?" Sure, sign now, ask questions later.

"Kiiids!" my dad calls up the stairs.

So now I have to go downstairs and act like everything is normal and my whole world didn't just cave in yesterday. Still, at least my family *are* quite a good distraction from that. They're a good distraction from pretty much everything really.

Ryan has his space helmet forcibly removed and as my dad dishes up the food Tammy starts telling Auntie Joan about the dog she is still trying to rescue.

"Well, I say just go for it," says Auntie Joan. "If you want something to happen, you have to *make* it happen. Wishing won't get results."

"Well, actually—" My mum starts to say something and then stops. She obviously doesn't entirely agree with this course of action, but doesn't want to start another fight.

"You reckon?" Tammy asks Auntie Joan. I notice she has conveniently not mentioned that she wants the dog to live with *us*, rather than *her*, once it's rescued.

"Absolutely," replies Joan. "*Just do it*, that's what I always say."

"Actually, I think that's the Nike slogan," I remark. My dad chuckles.

"They stole it from *me*," quips my aunt, and I laugh.

"Auntie Joan, did you really see Bigfoot?" asks Ryan then.

"Yes," says Joan. "It was amazing."

Then Joan tells us the story of a trip she went on a few years ago, to the Umatilla Indian Reservation in Oregon, where she and a few others think they definitely saw Sasquatch (which is apparently another name for Bigfoot).

I love my aunt's stories. Even though I know that this one lacks "any evidence at all" (according to my dad) because their footage is so dark and grainy, but my aunt still maintains she *knows what she saw*.

I hope one day I get to travel the world and see amazing things too.

Anyway, my parents consider our Sunday meal a raging success (largely because no one shouts, cries or storms out and they choose to ignore Ryan's mild griping about the lack of Kit Kats) so we all pat ourselves on the back and I am allowed to go upstairs and get on with my homework.

I'm supposed to be researching flowers online for the wildlife project. And I want to keep the goodwill with Natalie I've established this week, with all that bee and insect work we did. She's completely forgotten about the whole not-reading-*everything* debacle. And I want to keep it that way.

Unfortunately, as soon as I'm on my own again all I can think about is how angry and annoyed I feel with Scarlett. I can't *believe* she's just waltzed into the centre of my world and decimated it. I feel so impotent and powerless.

I *hate* her. And I'm very disappointed in Joshua. How can he be so taken in? She just dangles something his ego desires in front of him and bang, that's it. He's basically in her pocket.

Scarlett *can't* write for the comic, it's my *sacred*

place. This is like when the Nazis tried to get their hands on the Ark of the Covenant in the first Indiana Jones film. Or something. Except, you know, the comic won't kill us if we look at it.

Cartoons are *my* thing. *Mine*. They're the one thing *I* do that make other people like me. (Apart from Nat, who mainly likes me anyway. When I'm not annoying her.) They're the one thing that stops me feeling sad when someone is mean to me, because I can just turn them into a cartoon. They make me feel invincible. Kind of.

And *hello*? I'm clearly *good* at cartooning. That's why our comic is proving so successful. That's why for two issues in a row – 100% of the issues, in fact – the rest of the team wanted *my* pictures to be the front cover.

I co-write all of Tanya's quizzes; I help Joshua and Lewis brainstorm ideas; I help fix stuff that could be better; and I come up with loads of funny ideas all on my own. I'm *hilarious*. We don't need anyone coming in and "shaking things up" with their stupid ideas. Especially someone that hates me.

I know it might sound immature that I don't want there to be any *more* cartoonists, but I'd be *way* more happy to share if Scarlett wasn't such a horrible person. And if she hadn't been so mean and rude to me. And if she wasn't a thief or a compulsive liar. Call me picky if you like. *I* call it having standards.

There's *no way* the others will let her in. Tanya *hates* snobs. And Lewis hates thieves. Yeah, I have nothing to worry about. But, just to clinch it, maybe I should draw some cartoons now, just so it super looks like we don't need any more.

OK, I know I'm supposed to be doing this flowers research so that Natalie won't be mad at me, but I can just do that really quickly first.

Enthused, I look at the work sheet and start typing stuff into Google. I find a couple of websites that say things about pollution being bad, and bees and pollination. This all looks relevant. I bookmark the page.

I find a couple more likely-looking websites, then one that seems to be all about rare flowers specifically. The print is too small to read it all, and I'm itching to start drawing cartoons. So I take the laptop to the printer and just print everything I've found out to show Natalie at school. I can quickly go through it all by then anyway. It's probably easier to read on paper.

That done, I gleefully set about drawing some more sheep. And I should probably try to re-create the magic of the wasp/bee cartoon too. That went down well.

Ryan knocks on my door and asks to play Lego pirates but I tell him I'm too busy. I feel a bit bad when he looks upset. "I'm busy drawing cartoons, Ryan. We can't play at that together – it's not something you're interested in."

"I *am*," says Ryan defiantly.

"Are you?" I say sceptically. I don't have time for this.

"Yes," says Ryan. "Show me."

Then I have an idea. "OK, come here." On another pad, I draw a balloon. "See that? It looks flat, doesn't it?" Ryan nods. "You can make it look 3D if you draw this on it." And I add the kind of curved "window" bit that makes the balloon look round, and like light is reflecting off it.

"Cool," says Ryan.

"OK, you can practise doing that over there if you like. But I have to get on with this."

Ryan nods obediently and goes and sits cross-legged on my bed drawing balloons. Phew, that was easy.

Right. First I draw Mr Denton as a sheep. He teaches PE, so I draw him holding a basketball, wearing a "Baa-adidas" T-shirt (geddit?), and with a speech bubble saying, "I meant the other kind of dribbling!"

Then I draw a series of scenes featuring some sheep in unlikely situations, like queuing up in the school canteen and asking for more vegetables. I write captions under them and call this my "Things That Will Never Happen" series.

I get quite engrossed in what I'm doing and don't notice how much time has gone by. Blimey, it's later than I thought. Ryan's been quiet for a long time actually.

"Kids?" calls my dad up the stairs. "Are you getting ready for bed yet?"

"Yes!" I call back. It's not a *lie*, because my dad prefers the word *fib*. And I'm definitely *about* to start getting ready.

"Hey, Jess, look at this," says Ryan.

"Let's see then." I join him on the bed, expecting to see the fruits of his balloon labours, and indeed he has drawn many a balloon, but that is not what he wants to show me.

On a fresh piece of paper, scrawled in his six-year-old handwriting, are the words "Petishon Aboot Food". He's drawn some columns underneath, evidently without any kind of ruler judging by how wayward the lines are, then he's put his name, followed by a squiggle, which I imagine is what he thinks his signature would be.

It's simultaneously one of the daftest and cutest things I have ever seen, and I have to really try not to laugh in Ryan's face, as I'm genuinely impressed by the thought and ingenuity that has gone into this, however misguided and ultimately doomed his petishon might be.

Evidently Xylophone-gate was the last straw for Ryan and he is putting his foot down. "Confirmation Reaction," he explains.

Con *what*? Oh, wait a minute. This is the type of thing Tammy says when she's banging on about *her* petition. "Do you mean positive action?" I ask him.

(It's quite a big concept for Ryan.)

"Yes, positive action." Ryan nods, as if that was pretty much what he said and I'm just splitting hairs. "Tammy said make a stand on papers and Auntie Joan said just do it, so I'm doing it. They'll *have* to let us have Kit Kats now," he adds earnestly.

"I'm not sure that's quite how it works, Ryan," I say.

"Yes, it is: Tammy said," he says firmly. "You have to sign it."

"OK, Ryan," I say, taking the pad of paper from him and leaning it on my lap. "But to make it more official I'm adding this sentence: 'We the undersigned hereby declare that the policy of purchasing only Value food should be amended to allow for the inclusion of real Kit Kats.' And I'm going to put underneath: 'As you can see, 50% of the household disagree with the current policy and demand CHANGE.'"

"Yes!" Ryan beams and nods, as if he might have been about to suggest this too.

I hope my parents appreciate that it's the combination of Kit Kat deprivation with exposure to Tammy and Auntie Joan that has led to the radicalisation of their six-year-old child.

Chapter 15

So what has two thumbs and a load of excellent cartoons in their schoolbag? *This guy!* (You can't see me, but I am pointing at myself with my thumbs. Geddit? I don't think I will ever get bored of that joke.)

I'm practically bursting at the seams to show Joshua and the others my new stuff. I can't *wait* for our lunchtime comic meeting.

This briefly annoys Natalie at registration, as she wanted us to work on the project at lunchtime, but as I say to her (and stupid, *stirring* Amelia) I can do that *after* the meeting.

"Oh dear," says Amelia loftily. "Trouble in paradise?"

"Hardly," I retort. "There's plenty of time for everything."

"Good, good," lies Amelia. "Have you heard back from your experts yet?"

Some people in our class (like Cherry and Shantair, who *of course* wrote to wildlife experts on the *official* list) have had reply letters with all kinds of useful-looking booklets and information to help with their project.

"Yes, *actually*," says Natalie happily. "I wanted to show you at lunchtime, Jess. It's awesome; she's sent us all kinds of stuff."

"Oh great!" I enthuse. I hope it doesn't look bad that I haven't had a letter back yet.

"Have you?" Natalie asks Amelia.

"No," Amelia smiles, "but we've asked someone *very special* to help us, so I don't expect we'll hear back right away."

"Who?" I ask, unimpressed.

"Well, that would be telling," simpers Amelia.

Oh, who cares, Amelia? I manage not to shout. *Honestly.* And anyway, Natalie will forget all this

147

and be well impressed when she sees all the stuff about flowers that I printed off the Internet later.

"OK, so *new business*," says Tanya as we sit on the comfy seats outside the library at lunchtime. "Anyone?"

"I have some new business, actually," pipes up Joshua. *Me too, Joshua*, I think. *Me too.*

"And me." I manage to say this fairly normally.

"Jessica and I met this girl who wants to draw cartoons for our comic," says Joshua. "And, as Jess pointed out, she would have to be approved by everyone else too."

"Damn right," interrupts Tanya, nodding approvingly at me.

"So I've got her pictures here." Joshua reaches into his bag for some paper.

"Oh hey," I interrupt. "Can I do my new business first? It won't take a second."

"Go for it, Jess." Joshua gestures politely for me to have the floor, so I pass round my new cartoons to everyone.

Joshua really laughs at the Mr Denton one. (But

then he was the partial inspiration for it, telling me about his basketball practice.) I *love* making Joshua laugh. I don't know why. The others like them too, and everyone sort of chuckles.

"These are amazing," smiles Joshua.

"Bang-up job, Toons, as always," says Tanya.

"Yes, they're really good," agrees Lewis.

"Oh, good, I'm glad you like them." I try to sound casual. "They're just something I knocked up last night. But there *are* quite a lot of them. *Hang on* – you don't think…? And I'm just thinking aloud here, but maybe we don't have *room* for another person on the comic, if we have all these?" *Oh yeah, pretty subtle.*

Joshua shoots me a puzzled look. "OK, so," he says as he passes round some paper with various pictures of mice on them. "These are the cartoons this girl Scarlett drew, to see if we liked them. So what do you think?"

We all look at the mice pictures. I'm not very impressed by them. I mean, I suppose there's a chance I *might* be biased because I hate Scarlett so much. But honestly, I think they're boring.

It's just a series of mice with different slogans or

149

speech bubbles, like the one of a mouse holding a rucksack and it's saying, "School Sucks", which I'm sure is very *cool* and everything in cool-land. But our comic isn't cool-land. It's supposed to be funny. And as far as I can tell that cartoon is just an opinion, rather than an actual joke. It's empty.

"I don't like them," I say flatly. Might as well get the ball rolling.

"Well," Lewis pauses, looking at the pictures in turn, "I don't think they're *that* good."

"I sort of like them," says Tanya, "but I'm not that bothered."

"They're *OK*," amends Lewis, "they're just not brilliant."

"Three for three. Oh dear, it's unanimous," I say.

"Hang on, *I* like them," replies Joshua. I'm surprised at how these words cut me. It seems a bit ridiculous I could want Joshua only to like *my* cartoons and not those of my enemies but *still*. Ouch.

"Yeah, but you're outvoted," I inform him a bit sharply.

"You don't *run* the comic, Jessica," says Joshua, sounding annoyed.

"Nor do *you*," I retort.

"That's right, *I* do," jokes Tanya. "No, I'm just kidding. Trying to lighten the tension. You two need to sort it out; we've got work to do here."

"Yeah, well, Jessica should stop acting like she owns everything to do with *Hell*fern," snaps Joshua.

"Ha! That's rich coming from you!" I retort. "And I do actually do *loads* for this comic. More than any of *you*!"

"All right, careful there, Toons," says Tanya warningly. "Don't start getting big-headed for real."

"Sorry," I say, calming down and feeling faintly ridiculous.

"I just think it would be nice to give someone a chance," says Joshua flatly.

Well, it would be if they *deserved* a chance, I want to add, but don't. I feel like this argument has already gone too far.

"Well, it's causing too much drama," says Tanya. "Toons, you need to take a good look at yourself. Joshua, sorry, your new girlfriend can't be in the comic."

151

"She's not his *girlfriend*!" I blurt out. *Is* she? Why would I even care? I don't. I don't care. *Oh good grief.* Joshua doesn't answer the question. He just frowns and looks down.

"Tell you what, Joshy," says Tanya. "We'll have a look at her pictures again for the next issue. We've nearly got this one sorted; we're going to press soon, and we don't want to mess with a winning formula."

"Fine," mutters Joshua.

"So, can we agree on price? Twenty pence for the next issue?" Tanya moves business on briskly.

I hate the way Joshua keeps looking at me like he thinks I've been really mean, and sabotaged some innocent girl's chance of making it big in our comic. I start to *actually* feel guilty. I have to remind myself of all the unkind things Scarlett has said to me.

Maybe I should have told them about how nasty she is, and how she keeps trying to blank and bully me. And how she compulsively lies, and how she stole a soap from Boots. I'm slightly glad I *didn't* have to tell them about the soap because I once heard Tanya say that "snitches get stitches". But you know, *still*.

Joshua hasn't mentioned selling the comic in a comic shop though, which makes me think Scarlett hasn't been able to follow through on that promise, which again proves she *lies*, and I have done *nothing wrong*.

"Thanks for putting some of your lunch break aside to go over this stuff," says Natalie as I hand her my pile of Internet printouts on flowers in our form room, and she hands me her pile of booklets and literature from Diana Wood, a Wildlife Action committee member (whatever that is).

"My pleasure," I reply, pulling my chair closer to her desk. "This stuff looks amazing, you weren't kidding."

"I know," says Nat quite seriously. I thought she'd be more pleased by my compliment. "It's good to be cracking on," she continues, starting to rifle through my pile of paper. "We're going to need to pull something out of the bag if we want to do well at this, you know. Amelia finally told me who her *special* experts are."

"Who? Let me guess, the Queen?" I joke.

Natalie chuckles. "No, the *Cool For Cats* team."

"*What?*" I can't mask my scorn. "So, in other words, she's one of the people who are *never* going to get replies," I say. Those *idiots*. Not like me. I am definitely going to get a reply. Definitely.

"No, she's totally wangled it." Natalie lowers her voice, even though it is only us in the form room. "Remember her cousin, Scarlett?" *Oh no, here we go.*

"I'd rather not," I reply.

Nat chuckles again. "Well, she knows them somehow." Of course she does. She just knows every celebrity she wants.

"Let me guess, a friend's cousin?" I ask drily.

"Something like that. Anyway, she's taken Amelia's letter for her, and she's getting it right to them. Amelia and Cassy are going to have such an amazing project now." Natalie looks wistful.

I feel slightly tense as I wonder if Nat is wishing she'd gone with Amelia after all, to get this scoop. Then I remember that I don't believe it will happen because Scarlett is a serial liar, and I relax again. Weirdly, I feel a bit sorry for Amelia.

"Hey, you know what, Nat? Maybe you should tell

154

Amelia to write to some other experts as well, just in case?"

"Why?"

"I just don't trust Scarlett. I think she might be a bit of a liar."

"Really?"

"Yeah, you know… She said her belt was Prada, then she said it was Gucci. She said she was vegetarian, then Joshua and I saw her eat a hotdog… I just think Amelia should … hedge her bets." Nat lets out a small sigh. "What?" I ask.

"Jess, did you actually *read* this?" she asks tiredly, holding up a page for me to see.

"Yes, of course," I say defensively. "Well, most of it. Why?"

"Because you haven't printed out some information on wild flowers, you've printed out some information on a *band* called The Wild Flowers." I stare at her. "Rather than the actual plants?"

"What? Let me see that." I grab the paper off Natalie and study it properly. Oh no, she's *right*. Thinking about it, that does sort of explain why in the pictures the conservationists were looking a bit, you know, like goths. *Oh nooooooo*.

"I'm really sorry," I begin. "OK, I didn't read *that* bit, but I did read all the rest. You know, the stuff about the food chain bit, and the bees—"

"This is because you weren't concentrating properly, isn't it? It's because you were drawing all those stupid sheep for your stupid comic book, weren't you?" Natalie interrupts me crossly.

"What? Well, um," I stammer, unsure how to respond. That's kind of pretty much true.

"Oh look, Nat, I've drawn some amazing sheep. Look, aren't they great?" She does an impression of me from this morning, before registration. It's pretty accurate. "I *knew* you couldn't have drawn that many sheep and still got everything done."

"Hang on—"

"You keep choosing that immature comic over me and this project. Did you think I wouldn't notice? Are you *that* stupid?"

"I'm not stupid," I say, stung.

"That thing has really gone to your head, you know. You're *obsessed* with how many people like your pictures."

That's not true! Well. Kind of. Maybe it is a *bit* true. But even if it *is* true, I don't know why Nat would be so begrudging that I'm pleased my cartoons are popular. *Anyone* would be pleased by that. She and Amelia were so mean to me last term, I had to branch out. It's only natural that I would want to spend more time with people who like me than those who don't. That's not a *crime*.

"Well, this is just fantastic," says Natalie sarcastically. "Amelia is going to have the best project ever, thanks to Scarlett, and you're just sabotaging everything we do from within!"

And with that, Natalie grabs the pile of paper I'm holding, hoists her bag over her shoulder and storms out of our form room leaving me on my own.

The rest of the day goes by in a blur of annoyance. Natalie ignores me for ages, but by the time we need to get the bus home she is saying basic sentences to me again.

I feel guilty I didn't work harder on the project, but also really stung that she called me stupid. That's the sort of thing Amelia says, not Natalie.

I mean, sure, I'm not a high achiever *per se*, but I've got brains. All my report cards say so. They say I clearly have brains, but I don't tend to use them. *Hmmm.*

I'm not stupid. I still know the word inalienable.

I sulk in my room after dinner, unsure what I should do. Then I have a brilliant idea that will show Natalie I'm sorry I messed up, but in the *cleverest* way I know how. I will make a sorry card that makes me look *hyper-intelligent*.

I get a piece of card and fold it in half. First I draw a dolphin on the front (Natalie loves dolphins). It's the best dolphin I've ever done. I spend ages making it perfect and give it more details than I normally would. I leave a banner at the top, and colour the sea a bright blue and the dolphin grey with my felt tips. I'm going to write the words of the card in the banner at the top.

Then I go on to Google Translate and type in "I'm sorry" so it brings up the *Latin* (this is the crowning glory of my plan). Everyone knows you have to be super clever to know Latin. Or rich. Or learning a musical instrument. But *still*, it's impressive.

"I'm sorry" in Latin is "Paenitet". Which I guess kind of does look like the word "penitent" so maybe language does evolve and make sense, just like my dad claims it does.

Anyway, back to work. I use the online thesaurus to substitute fancy words I don't know for normal ones I do, to help me write a really intellectual message. So inside it says:

Dear Natalie, I'm veritably compunctious for upsetting you. I hope you can absolve me so we can be compatriots again, and culminate the wildlife project resplendently together. Yours, unfeignedly, unaffectedly, staunchly, steadfastly and dazzlingly, Jessica Morris Esq.

Oh yeah. How do you like me *now*? Who's stupid *now*? Exactly. Not me, that's for sure. I know all kinds of words. *In your face, haters*. Oh yeah. I *rock*.

Finally it is ready. I feel much better as I get into bed. I hope this brilliant idea works out better than my *secret* brilliant idea has so far.

Chapter 16

Tuesday starts really well. And that's probably the best thing that can be said about it.

I give Natalie the card in our form at registration and she really likes it.

"Oh my God, you didn't have to do that!" she exclaims, hugging me. "That's the best dolphin I ever saw! Wow, Jess! That's properly amazing!" She examines the card. "But what does it say?"

"Oh *that*?" I try to play it cool. "That's, uh, just some *Latin* I happen to know. It says I'm sorry, in Latin. Yeah, you know, I know stuff. Lots of stuff. I'm an asset to any team I'm on..." I trail off.

I might have come on a bit strong there, now I think about it. Not completely that subtle actually.

Natalie looks at me quizzically and opens the card. "What the— Jess? You are veritably compunctious?" She chuckles. "I don't know what that means, but I totally absolve you, and I want our project to be resplendent too!"

She hugs me again. "Oh, Jess!" she says, squeezing me really tightly. "I'm so sorry. By the way, I don't, never have and never will think you're stupid." She finally releases me. "And I'm really sorry if I gave you that impression. You don't have to prove you're clever to me."

"I don't know what you're talking about," I say evasively. "I totally just knew some Latin that I thought I'd throw in. No biggy."

Natalie chuckles. "Oh really?"

"Yes, really," I say. "I mean, I know you think I haven't been taking the project as seriously as you. I know you want a good mark and stuff. I'll work harder on it."

"I'm sorry I keep getting stressed about it," says Nat. "I do want it to be fun too. I think we're going to be fine."

"I *know* we are," I say. Though I can't help frowning as I notice that lots more people seem to

162

have had letters from their wildlife experts. Where's ours?

In the grand scheme of things, if it could have just stayed registration all day, everything would have been fine. I mean, whose idea was it to have *lessons* and stuff at school? Ludicrous.

Though, to be fair, my Tuesday morning lessons of double art and double English were perfectly OK.

I mean, I didn't *like* the way Joshua said he had a "major announcement" for the comic that he refused to reveal until our lunchtime meeting. But I liked the rest of art, and it was fun catching up with Megan, Emily and Fatimah. (Fatimah's five-year-old cousin in Manchester actually has a bouncy castle in his back garden – how lucky is that? Sometimes I wish I could be five on a bouncy castle again. Then I wouldn't have to deal with all this nonsense.)

I have a slightly sick feeling in my stomach as we all gather on the comfy seats outside the library at lunchtime. Tanya and Lewis seem genuinely excited and interested in whatever this new thing is, but I have a nasty suspicion about it.

"We have an offer to sell our comic in Big Dave's shop!" declares Joshua.

"*Yes!*" Lewis does a little air punch.

"Cosmic," says Tanya, looking composed, as if on some level she'd been waiting for this to happen. (I probably should have looked up what that actually means. But it sounds like it's a good and cool thing.)

"Oh right, that's, uh ... *happening*, is it?" I respond darkly. "There's no kind of ... *catch*, or anything, is there?" I ask, knowing full well what Joshua is about to say, but still hoping I'm wrong.

"Well, kind of, yes," says Joshua.

"We're not selling out and putting adverts in," says Tanya.

"No, it's not that," says Joshua. "Basically, Scarlett, the girl that wants her cartoons in the comic, has set this up at Big Dave's comic shop. It's kind of a *you scratch my back and I'll scratch yours* situation."

"Oh *right*," says Tanya. "So we put her in our comic, and she puts our comic in a shop? Like a business arrangement?"

"Yes," says Joshua. "And she wants to be on the front cover."

Noooooo! That crafty little… This is *outrageous*. And it doesn't even *count* as a front cover *win*, if she has to *bribe* her way into it. *Honestly*.

"I say we go for it," says Lewis. "Shall we vote?" *Noooooo!*

"All right, look," I hear myself say. "I didn't want to have to bring this up, but I think Scarlett is bad news."

"Oh, really?" Joshua folds his arms sceptically. "Nothing to do with you always wanting to be on the front cover?"

"Well—" I'm caught off guard. "I mean, I *do* think my bee cartoon is a better cover but that's not what—"

"That's not the issue, Toons," says Tanya.

"Look, she's *horrible*," I blurt out.

"Is she?" queries Tanya. "You never mentioned that before."

"Tanya, she's Amelia's cousin," I say.

165

"Ohhh."

"You can't judge someone on who their cousin is," says Joshua, which sounds annoyingly reasonable put like that.

"No, look, what I mean is," I struggle on. "She's been really mean to me. And also, I think she lies. I don't think we can trust her. I wouldn't be so sure this shop thing will really even *happen*. I think she just says things to get what she wants. And are we even ready for a shop anyway? We said we'd build a fan base at the school first."

"We were *born ready*, Toons," quips Tanya.

"OK, but look at the evidence, right. She said she was vegetarian at this sleepover, then Joshua and I saw her eat a hotdog. She said her belt was Prada then she said it was Gucci." (*Hmmm*, could it be that this all sounds a bit flimsy?) "And, you know when we were in Boots together? I saw her steal a soap!"

"Oh my God," says Joshua. "I see what's going on here." (*Finally!* Thank you.) "You're *jealous* of Scarlett!" *WHAT?*

"*What?*" I say. "No! If anything, she's jealous of *me*!"

"Well, why is it only *now* we're hearing about this

166

soap theft?" asks Joshua. "Why didn't you mention that sooner?" But it's hard to snap back and respond to him because I feel like I'm falling down a well.

"Look—" I attempt.

"It seems a bit convenient that Scarlett is *suddenly* a thief," continues Joshua. "I just find it very hard to believe you."

"Oh right, so *I'm* the liar!" I flare up at him. "Yeah, sure, why not. If that makes things easier for you, then fine!"

"Calm down, Toons," says Tanya.

"*No!*" I reply angrily. (I feel like I'm starting to have an out-of-body experience. Did I just *shout* at the scariest girl in school? Surely not.)

"Jess—" attempts Joshua.

"No!" I interrupt. "*Look.* I don't like this girl, and I say she doesn't get to go on the front cover just by bribing you idiots—"

"Who are you calling an idiot?" asks Tanya warningly, but I ignore her.

"I do *loads* for this comic!" I yell. "It would be *nothing* without me! You should *listen* to me on this!"

"OK." Tanya addresses the others calmly. "Toons has officially become a *nightmare*."

"Yeah," agrees Joshua, looking surprised. "You've got really arrogant, Jessica. I've never seen this side to you before."

"Look, if you include Scarlett's cartoons in the comic, I'm *quitting*." I can't believe I'm threatening them like this.

"That isn't making you look less arrogant, Jess," says Lewis. "Besides," he adds, "I don't get why you think we're not ready for this. You're normally the one that's all for world domination."

I am *all for world domination*, I think crossly. But Scarlett is *lying*! Why don't they believe me?

"I mean it, you guys," I say desperately, standing up and grabbing my bag. "Tanya, you wouldn't even *be* in this comic if it wasn't for me."

"Toons, I consider you a good friend, but you need to have a word with yourself," says Tanya flatly.

"Oh yeah, right," I says sarcastically. "Yeah, well, I suppose it's called *show-business* not *friend-business*!" (*Mental note: stop shouting at the scariest*

girl in school!)

"Don't be like this, Jessica," implores Lewis.

"Look, we're not going to be blackmailed by you, Jess," says Joshua. "We all contribute loads to this comic. It wouldn't be *nothing* without you."

"Fine then. I'll just go, shall I?"

"It's up to you, but we're not backing down from a democracy just because you've had a jealousy fit," he says. *Harsh!*

Don't cry, don't cry, I tell myself. I have to get out of here. I don't even do up my bag, I just run off, carrying it awkwardly. It doesn't make for the classiest getaway but that's the least of my problems now.

I manage to make it into a toilet cubicle before I start howling tears of rage and sadness. *How am I back here again? In a toilet, crying? How* has this happened? Eventually my sobs subside, and I start trying to calm down.

169

How has Scarlett got this far into destroying the glorious cartoon comic I was a part of, that made me think anything in the world was possible? *You know what? She's not worth it*, I sniff to myself.

But *somehow* she's succeeded. Despite not deserving to. This thought nearly makes me start crying again. *No*. I'm going to rise above it all. Somehow. Eventually. I blow my nose and wash my face.

Maybe Natalie's right and the comic had started to go to my head a bit. Well, I don't need people laughing at my cartoons to feel good about myself, like *Scarlett* obviously does. I've got *real* friends. Non "showbiz" ones, like Natalie, who like me for who I am. I wait a few more minutes till my face looks more normal and head back to my form room.

"Hey, Jess," says Nat happily. Yay! Someone's pleased to see me!

"I want a word with you," says Amelia.

"Hey!" I smile at Natalie. I forget I still haven't done up my bag, so as I heave it on to my desk the contents go everywhere. Natalie and Amelia help me pick everything up. It's mainly paper. Amelia seems distracted by some of it, then remembers she's annoyed with me.

"Natalie tells me you don't believe we're going to get the *Cool For Cats* team to write back to us," she says.

"Yeah, so?"

"So how dare you call my cousin Scarlett a liar!" she says. "My cousin is amazing and you owe her an apology."

HA! *Amazing.* Even if Scarlett apologised to *me* right now, that wouldn't change anything. "Well, it will be a cold day in hell before that happens," I tell her. "Your cousin Scarlett is one of the worst people I've ever met in my life. And I was trying to do you a favour, but *whatever.*"

"*Oh?*" Amelia is incensed. "You were doing *me* a *favour*, were you? You think honesty is so important? Well, maybe I'll do *you* a favour right now, shall I? Help you stop being such a hypocrite?"

"What are you talking about?" I ask, confused.

Amelia suddenly flings a piece of paper under Nat's nose. "Here you go, Jessica. Let's show Natalie this letter that just fell out of your bag, shall we? Perhaps *you* can explain *that* for us?"

"What the—" begins Nat. I look at the piece of

paper. It's the letter I wrote to the official wildlife person and then never posted – because I had a brilliant *secret surprise* idea instead.

"You didn't post your letter?" cries Nat. "Were you *ever* going to tell me?" Her voice rises, sounding hurt. "We're waiting for someone to write back, who is *never* going to?"

"It's not what you think," I say. But I sort of don't have the energy to deal with this right now. "Look, Nat, I've had a really bad day, I can explain exactly what—"

"Did you send another letter to this guy then? Was this just a practice?" Nat interrupts.

"Well, no, but—"

"I rest my case," says Amelia smugly.

"You can't rest your case. You don't know anything about the case," I snap, annoyed.

"I knew this would happen," says Nat. (What did she know would happen?) "You're slack and make loads of mistakes because you're too distracted by your stupid ego-trip comic."

172

"Well, you don't need to worry about that any more," I murmur.

"Yeah, you're right. I should just give up now and resign myself to this F, shouldn't I?" says Nat sarcastically.

"No, look, Nat, I have a secret surprise about this." I'm just going to have to tell her and hope for the best.

"What secret surprise?"

"OK. I didn't want to tell you until … OK. I *did* send a letter."

"Oh no." Some kind of penny drops inside Nat's head. "To *who*?"

"To Horace King, the wildlife bird guy," I say.

Natalie does a dramatic yet sarcastic face-palm movement.

I continue anyway. "I figured no one else would write to him, so there was a good chance he'd reply." (And I wanted to cheer my dad up into the bargain.) "I didn't tell you because I wanted it to be a surprise when a cool letter just showed up." (Also, I thought there was a *chance* you'd react like this, I don't add.) "So … uh … surprise!" I finish dejectedly.

"And has he written back?" asks Amelia cruelly.

"Not *yet*," I reply defiantly.

"Oh, Jessica," says Nat sadly. "He's *never* going to write back! What were you *thinking*? You've *ruined* our project!"

"Well, you weren't letting me make any of the decisions!" I fire back spontaneously. (Where's *this* coming from?) "Everything's on *your* terms. We've done the whole project how you wanted it. I can't even tell you anything without you getting angry. What about what I want?"

Then suddenly Nat looks *really* angry. "*I wish I'd never gone with you!*" And she storms out of the form room. For the second time in two days.

"*Favour repaid*," smiles Amelia.

Amazingly, I don't burst into tears.

Chapter 17

I'm not saying it's the worst Tuesday anyone's ever had, but— No, wait, actually I *am* saying that. That's *exactly* what I'm saying. *Worst Tuesday EVER.* Officially. I hate everyone and everything.

I kick stones aggressively down the path as I mooch my way home after school. The frustrating thing is, I don't actually feel like I've done anything *that* wrong, so I don't know what I can change to make it better.

Normally I can at least formulate a plan. This time I've got nothing. I mean, OK, I didn't send that letter to the *official* person but I did it for the *right reasons*. I'm still brilliant, and even brilliant people make mistakes. In a way Natalie is *lucky* I'm so brilliant I can admit this. *Ohhhh.*

Is it true? Have I become unbearably arrogant? Did I overreact to the whole Scarlett cartoon thing? I mean, if I had less ego I could have just graciously let her be on the cover and I'd still be in the comic … *ohhhhh.* No, there's a principle at stake. She's evil. They'll learn.

I wish I had a time machine. Then I could go back in time and post that letter. And not go to Amelia's sleepover, so that I'd never meet Scarlett. I wonder how far off time travel is? I doubt it will be ready in time to help me with this.

"Here's your capitalist washing," says my mum, handing Tammy a neatly folded pile of clothes. "*Muggins here* finished it off for you."

"And muggins *here* made cauliflower cheese," my dad pipes up, putting a sizzling dish in the centre of the table.

"And muggings here laid the table," adds Ryan, sitting down.

176

Really, I think we need to eradicate the nickname *muggins*, not spread it round further. I sit down. Mind you, if everyone uses it like this, maybe it will lose all sense of meaning and my mum will have to think of something else to call herself.

I mean, if my mum is just *trying out* the nickname muggins, that's fine. It's her business. As long as she eventually realises it's annoying and stops. But I still think it's attention-seeking behaviour.

"This looks pretty good, Bert," says my aunt, in a rare moment of praise for my dad, also sitting down at the table.

Once all the food is dished up, Ryan clears his throat, a bit dramatically. "I have an announcement," he says.

"Well, don't let your food get cold," says my dad.

Ryan ignores this lacklustre response, pulls a piece of paper out of his pocket and unfolds it for everyone to see. "This is very serious," he says. "Mummy, please take this and read it aloud," he instructs pompously.

Curiously, my mum starts reading. "Petishon?" She raises an eyebrow at his spelling. "We the undersigned... What is this, Ryan?"

"It's a petition," says Ryan. "You have to read it, Mummy."

My mum dutifully starts to read. "We the undersigned hereby declare that the policy of purchasing only Value food should be amended to allow for the inclusion of real Kit Kats. As you can see, 50% of the household disagree with the current policy and demand CHANGE."

Auntie Joan and Tammy look like they are trying not to laugh. My mum hands the paper to my dad. Ryan looks at them expectantly. "I'm effecting action, like Tammy, and *just doing it*, like Auntie Joan," he explains.

"And Nike," I can't help but add.

"This is what we *anti-capitalists* call 'Fat Cats marketing to children so that they recognise branding and pester their parents for it'," says Tammy smugly. "They actually do call it *pester power*. Looks like there's a downside to mass corporations after all. Who knew?"

I suppose Tammy must have been finding it difficult to keep up her various campaigns *and* maintain access to the washing machine, so this is a nice little gift for her.

"Please can we have Kit Kats now?" asks Ryan.

"Well, Ryan." My dad is the first to find his voice. "Your mother and I will review the current policy and get back to you. How about that?"

"Spoken like a true politician," remarks Tammy.

"What does that mean?" asks Ryan.

"They'll think about it," I say.

"*Nooo*, now," whines Ryan, but wisely sensing this particular battle is over, he starts eating his dinner.

I'm moping in my room when Ryan comes in later, wanting to play Lego pirates again. I couldn't be less in the mood, but I'm aware I turned him down last time he wanted to play, so I say yes and then slump on to the floor while he goes and gets them all.

It's a continuation of the same story with the first mate Clyde being kidnapped, but now someone else – an impostor – has pretended to be Clyde, so he can infiltrate the gang and mess things up.

I start to get quite interested in this storyline. "What's going to happen, Ryan?" I ask, slightly more on the edge of my seat than I realised.

"There'll be an ambush here, and then we fire these

cannon here, and—"

"No, I mean with Clyde and the impostor. Does it have a happy ending?"

"Oh," Ryan shrugs. "Yeah, I guess."

"What happens?" I demand, a tiny bit too intensely, now I think about it. But how can he be so callous about these Lego pirates' *lives*?

"Oh, well, Calzo the impostor gives himself away," explains Ryan. "Not yet though. But he's bad at pretending, so he ruins it. First we need to do this ambush—"

"I love you, Ryan," I blurt out. I can't express better than that how this Lego pirate storyline is music to my ears.

Seriously, considering how Ryan spends most of his time behaving like a hyperactive hooligan, his moments of quiet wisdom are all the more amazing.

"Yeah, yeah," says Ryan dismissively, as if that goes without saying.

We play Lego pirates and I take particular delight when Calzo is finally made to walk the plank. Ha! *Yeah, take that, Scarlett/Calzo*, I think.

I haven't gone insane, honest.

But there's just something very calming about a story where a bad guy gets their comeuppance (and is eaten by Lego sharks) when a similar (more cartoon and less Lego-based) thing has happened to you.

I just feel better. I feel like I have things in perspective more. Let them all follow Scarlett to this shop. Let her carry on. She'll blow her cover and accidentally reveal all the lies she's been telling sooner or later. She's not even a particularly good liar. Give her enough rope to hang herself and let her get on with it. *I'll* be fine.

When Ryan leaves to get ready for bed, and I'm no longer distracted by pirate vengeance, I realise I'm still upset about Natalie though. And I don't think Ryan will have any good solutions to that problem. *Hmmm*, I sigh.

I sit at my desk and go through all the work we've done so far. I feel sad as I look at the pages of all the leaves we correctly identified, and the things we did well together. How did it come to this?

Finally I come to the chapter in the book on wildlife animals. There's a picture of a badger. I like this badger for some reason. It looks quite cute, and yet kind of serious. I start reading the chapter.

Wow, it turns out that badgers are really cool. Well, you know, maybe not *cosmic* exactly, but certainly not to be messed with. When protecting their young, badgers can fight off much larger animals, like wolves and bears! And they can run at nearly twenty miles per hour for short periods of time. That's really quite fast.

There's been debate about hunting badgers over the years. They've been protected by the 1935 Cruelty To Animals Act and the 1992 Protection of Badgers Act, but now the book says something about how that might change again. I can't believe anyone would want to hurt these little creatures. I wish they could always be protected by some laws.

I look at the picture again. The badger is looking at the camera. This might sound weird, but it's kind of like the badger is looking at me. I start feeling like I have some kind of connection with it. Like I, too, have been hunted for sport, by Amelia and, to a lesser extent, Scarlett. (Maybe I *have* gone mad after all?)

We haven't drawn any pictures at all yet for the project, under Natalie's strict instructions. I could always draw this badger. I mean, we are going to need *some* pictures. I know my reputation is that I get carried away with stuff and do too much drawing before we've finished the proper work (or in my case usually before I've really *started* the actual work). But we've kind of done quite a lot of the work this time.

Also, Natalie isn't talking to me, so it's not like I can ask her opinion on it anyway. *Ohhh.* She said she wished she'd never gone with me. Well, you know what? I wish I'd never gone with *her*. I had other offers (admittedly from people that I've now also fallen out with). *Hmmm.* Maybe the problem *is* me.

No. It isn't. I'm nice and brilliant, and I mean well. And if other people can't see it, that's *their* problem. I suddenly feel angry and vindicated. Picturing Natalie telling me not to do this for some reason spurs me on further.

And you know what else? Natalie was so worried about "pulling something out of the bag" to compete with Amelia, some kind of big finish. Well, I am going to make this really big. Yeah. I'm going to draw a sarcastically big badger. That'll show her.

I open my new giant pad of paper, the same size as the one I used to draw the giant Easter bonnet last term. I sit and look at the badger a bit longer, soaking in every detail. And then I start drawing.

An hour later, I realise that it's going to take longer than I thought. Because I want to do the badger picture so carefully it ends up taking me a really long time to just sketch out the shape with my pencil. I want it to be really good. I'm not going to finish this tonight. My hand is starting to hurt. I'll have to finish it tomorrow.

But as I sit back and look at what I've done I feel really pleased. It's the most accurately-like-the-thing-I'm-trying-to-draw thing I have ever succeeded in drawing. I don't want to rush it and ruin it. I want it to be as brilliant as it can be.

Then it dawns on me that this picture is no longer an attempt to get revenge on Natalie. That might have been how it started, and that energy might have fuelled it in the beginning, but somewhere along the way I started caring about making a brilliant picture for the sake of it.

I'm not even completely sure what I was thinking about when I was doing some of it. But I feel a lot calmer and happier and more complete now that I have finished half of it. I feel lighter. Like a weight has been lifted. Maybe I'm not mad after all. This really is how drawing makes me feel.

I'm so glad drawing is my secret super-power. And Scarlett can never take that away from me. Maybe it's time to put *operation-calm-down-and-stop-overreacting* into motion. *Maybe*.

Chapter 18

Wednesday is pretty uneventful. Natalie ignores me and I hang out with Cherry and Shantair at break time and lunch. I avoid everyone from the comic and they avoid me. I assume. I mean, I'm not looking for them, so it's hard to tell for sure.

I can't help but think that not speaking is unhelpful when you need to get a wildlife project done though. So I decide to ignore Nat ignoring me, and at the end of lunch I go up to her and ask how we are going to divide up the remaining chapters in our finished project book (and also how we are going to work on the presentation if we aren't even speaking).

She just gives me this look and says, "Do whatever you want. You will anyway." Which is even more unhelpful in some ways.

But at least it gives me some annoyance to channel when I get home from chess club and finish my badger picture. It looks *amazing* now. I think it might be the best picture I've ever drawn.

I even start wondering if maybe it is a valid contribution to the project after all. Part of me thinks that by doing this (and doing it well) maybe I am helping rectify the damage I caused. Maybe Natalie will even be slightly impressed. It makes me feel better, like I am contributing in some way, and making the project less of a disaster.

I'm more nervous as I enter school on Thursday, because I know today is when the second issue of the comic is published. I assume everyone went round to Lewis's last night to help fold all the printouts in half. I kind of don't want to see this issue of my ex-comic.

Natalie comes over to my desk at registration. "I, um," she says, "I'm sorry. For ignoring you yesterday and for how I spoke to you the other day. I might have overreacted."

"Really?" I say, surprised. I didn't think she would ever forgive me. I mean, the evidence is still *kind of* that I ruined our project by writing to Horace King. But I suppose she was quite harsh to me too.

"I made you some dinosaur cookies to say sorry properly," says Natalie, producing a small Tupperware box.

"I *love* dinosaur cookies," I reply, touched.

"Friends?" asks Nat.

"OK." We both smile awkwardly.

"Thank goodness." Nat launches herself on to my desk and starts gabbling. "I am so sorry, Jess. I've been acting like a complete monster. I'm really glad we've gone together on the project, and I'm sorry I said I wasn't. I didn't mean it."

"No, *I'm* really sorry," I say. "You were right, *I've* become a monster about the comic. I got obsessed with it, and I should have put the project first more often. I've been reading loads of the books now though. I've got lots of ideas for the presentation." Then I play my trump card. "And I drew a brilliant picture of a badger. Do you want to come round to my house tonight and see it?"

"I would like nothing more," says Nat, beaming.

"And I'm off the comic anyway, so that won't get in the way now either," I add.

"I, er, heard about that," says Nat. "Are you OK?"

"Oh yeah, I don't care any more," I lie and wave a hand dismissively. "Water off a duck's back now."

I think Nat is about to probe further on this and discover that I am only pretending to have this blasé attitude, but then Amelia kind of stalks past us and slumps on to her desk, looking upset.

Nat and I exchange looks. I nod at her. "Um?"

Nat addresses Amelia kindly as we go over to her. "Is everything OK?"

"Not really," says Amelia sulkily.

"Do you want to talk about it?" offers Nat.

"Scarlett got caught shoplifting last night," says Amelia.

"No way!" cries Nat.

"Blimey," I comment.

"Yeah." Amelia sighs. "And stuff has gone *missing* from our house," she adds in a low voice. "And Scarlett is kind of the only one who could have taken it."

"Oh, Amelia, I'm really sorry," says Natalie.

"That's awful."

"Yeah," I agree. Though part of me wants to shout *I TOLD YOU SO!* at the top of my voice. *No*, that was the *big-headed* Jessica of the past; now I am kind and calm. And probably compassionate.

"Scarlett went through a bit of a stealing-phase when her parents first got divorced," says Amelia wearily, "but everyone thought she'd stopped."

"That's kind of sad," I say. And I realise that I mean it. I didn't picture Scarlett as *unhappy*; I just thought she enjoyed being mean and pretentious for the sake of it. All this time it was a cry for help.

And I feel sorry for Amelia. Even after what she did to me with the letter. She loves her cousin loads and is very protective of her. It must be devastating to find out something like this about someone you look up to so much.

I'd hate it if my aunt or my sister got arrested. Though actually, thinking about it, they both have. But you know, not for *bad* crimes, just for criminal damage and obstructing demolition lorries and stuff. Not for stealing.

No, I shake my head. I mustn't start feeling *too* sorry for Amelia or Scarlett. They can both still be horrible. But I don't feel as angry with either as I did, and we head off to class.

For once I'm not looking forward to double art. This is mainly because (a) I haven't spoken to Joshua since I stormed out of our meeting, and (b) Terry, Emily, Megan and Fatimah all have copies of issue two of the comic, which I still don't want to see.

But as I take my seat at our table, I decide if I really want to become a nice, non-big-headed monster, I should probably try and be the bigger person. Maybe try and make amends somehow.

"All right?" says Joshua gruffly, by way of testing the water. He takes his seat next to me.

The others are just pointing and giggling at their favourite bits of the comic, so they don't notice or comment on any tension between us.

"Hi," I say. "I want to apologise to you for storming out of the comic and overreacting about Scarlett's cartoons." I state this amicably.

"Really?" asks Joshua, clearly surprised.

"Yes," I say. "It's come to my attention that I *might* have turned into a bit of a fame-hungry-monster, and so I'm sorry about that."

"Wow," says Joshua. "You never seem to stop surprising me." (I resist the urge to make a joke about how great I am because I'm  full of surprises as this might undermine my earlier statement.) "So you're not annoyed about Scarlett being in the comic?" asks Joshua.

"Well—" I begin, but he interrupts.

"Because I'm meeting Scarlett at the weekend, and we're going to go to the comic shop and—"

"I don't think you are." It's my turn to interrupt him.

"Excuse me?" says Joshua.

"Um, the thing is, I don't Scarlett will make it. She's mega-grounded, apparently. She got caught shoplifting last night."

"You're not *serious*?" exclaims Joshua in a low voice.

"I heard it from Amelia. It's true," I state.

Joshua considers this for a moment. "Then I guess I owe *you* an apology too. For not believing what you said about her."

192

Well, yes, *damn straight you owe me an apology,* I think. "Apology accepted," I say. We shake hands.

"So I take it you're back in the comic then?" asks Joshua.

"Hey, Jess, I *love* the quiz this week!" exclaims Emily. "*Which Reality TV Star Are You?* I'm the one that keeps attacking taxi drivers! Ha ha."

And as she waves the comic at me, I look up and see that Scarlett's "School Sucks" mouse cartoon has made the front cover.

Ouch. I blink. It still hurts. Even though I *knew* this had probably happened. And even though I *said* I would be the bigger person and stop letting my ego get carried away.

"Oh, you put her on the front cover?" I manage to say quietly to Joshua.

"Yes," says Joshua. "So you're back in?"

"I need to think about it."

Emily, Megan and Fatimah talk lots about how much they love my bee cartoon (which has made the *back* cover, sharing the space with the fake gossip about teachers) and it does cheer me up a bit. But *still*. And anyway, I can't put all my self-esteem eggs in one cartoon basket. Any more.

Having said that, Natalie *loves* my badger picture! I knew she would. We sit in my kitchen eating what's left of her dinosaur biscuits and admiring it. "It's definitely the best thing you've ever done," she repeats. "This definitely makes up for the fact that you wrote to some mad, old bird guy," she teases, crunching into another dinosaur.

"*Oi!*" I pretend to hit her.

"Oh sorry, were you not ready to laugh at that yet? It's kind of funny," giggles Nat, finishing her cookie.

"Don't fill up on those," says my mum, entering the kitchen. "I'm starting dinner now. I assume you're staying, Natalie poppet? It's not very exciting, I'm afraid." Before Nat can answer, my mum carries on, "And, Jess, have you picked up your post yet? It'll get lost in this house if you don't."

"I didn't know I even *had* post," I say, going to retrieve it from the hallway and coming back. It's a bulky brown envelope. I rip it open and pour the contents on to the kitchen table.

It looks like an information pack of some kind,

with photographs and booklets. There's a covering letter on top, with a familiar logo in the corner.

I pick up the letter. Suddenly I recognise that one of the photographs is an owl being held by … none other than Horace King! "Oh my *God*!" I exclaim. No *WAY*! *He wrote back?* I start reading the letter.

"What?" Natalie jumps up and starts trying to read over my shoulder.

"It's a letter from … Horace," I manage.

"No way! He wrote back? What does it say?"

I start reading the letter. "It says, 'Dear Jessica and Natalie'—" I break off. "That's us!"

"I know!" squeals Natalie. "Carry on."

" 'I was utterly delighted to receive your letter about your wildlife project.' Wow! He was *delighted*!"

I read on. Horace's letter says that wildlife conservation is an issue really close to his heart, and so he is *thrilled* that young people are taking an interest in it. (I mean, in all fairness we were forced to by our school, but let's not focus on that for now.)

He says normally the people that write to him are middle-aged (like my dad, I guess!).

And because he's so over the moon that some young people wrote to him, he says he would like to invite us to the bird sanctuary he is a patron of, to meet some of the rescued birds and animals! Including Poppy, a barn owl who was recently on *Blue Peter*. If that would help us with our project? This is *amazing*.

"Uh, Nat, just tell me again how I ruined our project by writing to that mad, old bird guy?" I say.

"I'm sorry, I'm sorry!" Nat is incredulous. "I never thought – I'm sorry. I was wrong."

"And I was right?" I prompt, enjoying myself.

"Yes," says Natalie tiredly.

"Say it."

"You were right."

"Hang on, say it again, I want to record it—"

"Oh, shut up!" laughs Nat. "You're totally amazing, I'm totally an idiot etc etc. There. Gloating done.

This is *amazing*, Jess!"

"Hey, the gloating will be done when I say it's done," I say. "But yes, this is amazing!" Nat and I hug and jump up and down with excitement.

"What's all this then?" asks my dad, entering the kitchen.

I hand him the letter and he goes quiet for a moment as he reads it. I thought he might show more of a reaction than this, to be honest. I mean, it's his childhood hero for crying out loud.

Finally my dad clears his throat. "Now, Jessica, I'm afraid you're just a bit too young to go off and do things like this on your own." I look at him, starting to feel crushed. "So I think I'm just going to have to come with you." Then his face cracks into a massive grin and he nearly starts jumping up and down as well. "Horace King! I can't believe it."

My brilliant secret plan has actually worked out *perfectly*. Like, to the *letter*. See? I don't need a comic to make me feel good. I am a nice friend, sister and daughter. I can be brilliant in non-big-headed ways. I don't need any further approval. (Admittedly, saying it like that sounds slightly big-headed, but *still*.)

Chapter 19

The bird sanctuary is a lot of fun. Nat and I both feel a bit nervous when we first arrive, as we're not sure what to expect.

"We've got to be brave," whispers Nat. "And besides, I bet none of our classmates have come here."

"Well, you know, they didn't have *genius little me* in their teams, to think of writing to the right people."

Nat rolls her eyes. "You know what I mean. And I bet they haven't got anything like this close to any celebrities."

"Can we call him a celebrity?" I ask.

"He is to your dad."

We wait in the foyer until we hear the receptionist

say, "Your guests are here, Horace."

Then Horace steps out, "Hello, hello!" he says jovially.

My dad bounds up to him, way too eager. "It is an *honour* to meet you, sir," he says. I feel slightly embarrassed by how keen my dad is. And why did he have to call him *sir*?

"Nonsense!" Horace shakes my dad's hand warmly.

I think my dad must be nervous too, because then he says, "I've liked you since I was seven." Then he adds, quite unnecessarily, "I'm forty-eight now."

Luckily Horace looks amused. Natalie and I try and stifle our giggles.

Horace smiles at us. "And you must be Natalie and Jessica?" We nod shyly. "I loved your letter." We smile. "So. Are you ready for a crazy old man to show you some birds?"

Natalie and I can't help but giggle. "Yes," I manage.

"Please," says Natalie.

Horace waves his hand jauntily and motions that we should follow him.

After five minutes of talking to Horace, Natalie and I decide he's not crazy at all, just very enthusiastic about birds. He's also very funny and completely self-aware. He seems to actively delight in playing up to a slightly eccentric image.

Horace shows us around the sanctuary, chatting knowledgeably about all the different birds. He tells us how he was about our age when he first got interested in birds and learned to identify all the different types in his garden by their different songs and plumages.

He says what sounds like simple birdsong to us is actually amazingly complicated and contains all sorts of different systems and meanings, and he talks about the zebra finch and how if it doesn't hear its species' mating call within the first eighteen days of its life, it can never learn it, and can then never mate. (Which seems like quite a heavy price to pay for being in the wrong place at the wrong time.) Horace laughs delightedly when I say this.

Then he shows us how to make a bird feeder for our gardens. My dad gets ridiculously excited by this because it's a lot like the one he made as a child, when he tried to copy the way Horace did it on TV. So Horace lets my dad make one to take home as well, and he is all smiles. *Honestly*.

At the end we have our photographs taken with Horace and Poppy the barn owl from *Blue Peter*. By this point my dad is having such a good time that he doesn't appear even slightly embarrassed when he asks if he can get his picture taken with Poppy and Horace as well. He's like a giant, gleeful five-year-old. But Horace happily obliges.

Despite my dad's antics, this bit is really exciting. I feel scared as they lower the bird on to my arm, which is covered by a special glove. It's terrifying, but also thrilling. And for ages afterwards the adrenalin is going nuts inside me.

We part company with Horace happily, agreeing with him about the dangers of global warming and promising to buy some energy-saving light bulbs for our house. All in all, it's an amazing experience.

I was right about my dad loving meeting Horace. He's been on cloud nine since we got home. I think he sort of might actually want to *be* Horace. My cunning plan to cheer him up may have worked *too* well.

"I want to replace all our old light bulbs with energy-saving ones straight away," he announces, sitting down to that night's dinner of *Super Saver Value* spaghetti bolognese.

My mum looks at him suspiciously. "Have you been talking to Tammy? Did she put you up to this?"

"No," says my dad. "Horace King said—"

"Oh no, not Horace King *again*," interrupts my mum. "I'm *sick* of hearing about him all the time."

"Mum, to be fair, we've only been back two hours," I say.

"Well, it feels like longer," snaps my mum.

"What?" objects my dad. "Jessica and I had a wonderful time at his sanctuary. And it will not only help the planet, but it will save us money. I was reading online and it could save us up to three pounds a year per bulb!"

"Oh, it will be way less than that," my aunt assures him. "You hear all kinds of conflicting amounts with these things."

"The point is, there'll be savings," says my dad.

"I vote for Daddy," pipes up Ryan.

"What do you mean, you vote for Dad?" I say. "No one's even voting on anything."

"I vote for Daddy's savings, and then with the money we save we can buy Kit Kats again," explains Ryan.

"*Plus ça change, plus c'est la même chose*," says my aunt absently.

"What does that mean?" asks my dad.

"The more things change the more they stay the same," I reply, suddenly realising I know it. "It's French." So *that's* how the rest of that saying goes. I have just applied learning to an everyday situation. Amazing. This must be how properly clever people feel every day.

"Vote for the Kit Kats! Vote for the Kit Kats!" Ryan tries to start up a chant.

"So you're saying Ryan is repetitive?" comments my mum drily.

"Vote for the Kit Kats!"

"You know what, I vote for the Kit Kats as well," I say. "Just for the sheer determination involved."

"Well," says my mum. "If we're *saving* money on

electricity, we can … possibly afford to start buying Kit Kats again."

"Yesssss!" shouts Ryan, punching the air with his fist.

"Next saving we make, muggins here is getting a new wing mirror!" *Enough with the nickname, Mum!*

"You need a new wing mirror?" my aunt says to my mum, sounding surprised.

My mum laughs. "Did you think the gaffer tape was part of some used-car chic we were going for?"

My aunt laughs too and rolls her eyes.

"I'm sorry, love, we can't stretch to that yet," says my dad sadly.

"Kit Kats! Kit Kats! Kit Kats!" chants Ryan, completely oblivious to my mum's woes.

"But the lesson here is managing your budget," my dad tells Ryan pointlessly.

I don't think that is the lesson Ryan will be taking away from this experience at all. I think he views the lesson as: never-shut-up-about-Kit-Kats-and-you-will-win.

So what has two thumbs and a load of Kit Kats?

Ryan does! (Come on, guys, sometimes you have to subvert the formula; keep up.)

Natalie and I are spurred on by meeting Horace and seeing all those birds up close. His enthusiasm for the subject is infectious and we decide to do a load of work on our project in an inspired flourish, writing the chapter on birds together the next day, while it's still fresh in our minds.

I spend so much time with Nat over the next week, doing our wildlife work, that I don't really have time to think much about the comic. The sting of Scarlett making the front cover has faded, and now I feel faintly ridiculous I could have cared so much about it. Maybe it's been good for me to have a break from it, and become less egotistical.

Nat and I have agreed to keep our trip to the bird sanctuary a secret so that we have an exciting ace up our sleeves in the presentation. The presentations are coming up really soon now; it's getting a bit scary.

My usual tactic when something scary is looming is to ignore it. But that gets difficult if you live next door to the VanDerks, and the thing you are avoiding is vaguely academic.

"Ah, here's young Jessica!" calls Mr VanDerk the following Monday as I walk up my garden path after school and see him chatting to my mum over the hedge. "How's it going with the presentation preparation? Are you nervous?"

"She's been working very hard," my mum answers for me as I draw level with them.

"Harriet's not nervous at all," says Mr VanDerk. "But then she's used to public speaking, of course. She's form captain and part of an outside-school debating society."

"Well, Jessica's got … *good instincts*," says my mum, as always trying to compete in this unwinnable competition. "Don't you, Jess?"

"Oh yes," I agree. And right now my instinct is to get inside the house, away from this nonsense.

Just then the sound of an engine revving and a thumping car stereo attracts our attention. We look over as Auntie Joan pulls up in my mum's car and rolls down the window.

"Coo-eee!" she yells, then switches the engine off and gets out.

"What have you done to my car?" cries my mum,

206

running down the path. I follow, as does Mr VanDerk.

"Well, I went to get the wing mirror fixed, to say thanks for cooking me all these meals and everything," explains Joan, "and while I was there I thought I'd get some other changes made as well."

"You don't say?" My mum gapes open-mouthed at her car.

"So now it's also got a brand-new stereo with a digital radio, loads of speakers, UV lights, built-in satnav, and cup holders. Oh, and new tyres. These ones can go off-road if you need them to. Pretty groovy, hey?"

"And what's with the flames down the sides?" I ask.

"Oh, them? The guy just threw them in for free," says my aunt. "I think he wants to be a graphic designer really."

"Where on earth did you—" My mum can't even finish her sentence, she's too gobsmacked.

"This car looks like it's owned by a boy racer," remarks Mr VanDerk stiffly.

"It looks like Greased Lightning," I comment.

And then, just when I think my mum's head is going to explode, she bursts out laughing. She laughs and laughs. She doubles over and has to wipe tears from her eyes before she is able to stop. Then she hugs Joan.

"You're a complete nutcase," she tells her sister. "What would I do without you?"

"Drive inconspicuously?" I offer. But this just makes them laugh more.

Chapter 20

"Harriet VanDerk and Amy White," calls out Miss Price. They are the first ones up. All of Year Six are sitting here in the hall, feeling pretty nervous. *It's presentation day, it's presentation day.*

Some people from the Wildlife Association Council have joined our teachers as judges and to give out any prizes and stuff. It makes the event feel kind of official and sombre.

When Harriet and Amy finish, we all applaud politely and Mrs Cole says Harriet has "set the bar high". Then she gets the next team up.

The next few presentations aren't quite as thorough as the first. Megan and Emily didn't have half those facts, and for some reason they talked loads about going on a bike ride and really enjoying the scenery. They say we should protect the environment so other people can go on bike rides, which I agree with, but it just sounds less official somehow.

Cherry and Shantair, my chess club friends, have loads of really great information, but Cherry kind of mumbles and looks down when she speaks and so it's hard to catch everything she says. Shantair is really shy too, even though she does drama. She did once tell me that she hates talking in front of people and that part of the reason she does drama is to try to overcome her fear.

Joshua and Lewis somehow manage to link their project to Dracula (don't ask) and various comic book characters. They mention the Black Mercy flower putting Superman to sleep and Captain Carrot, an ordinary rabbit, eating carrots that were struck by lightning and then becoming a superhero.

They ponder if garlic could really repel a vampire, but then cleverly link it to real life, when they say that destroying the rainforest means we are destroying loads of potential future medicines in the undiscovered plants. It isn't exactly in the remit of what we were completely supposed to do, as it's not really *local* wildlife, but it is definitely the most interesting presentation, and my favourite so far.

Cassy and Amelia have lots of thorough and impressive information, but the *Cool For Cats* team never wrote back (probably because they never got a letter in the first place) so I think they might get marked down for not doing everything that was asked. I still feel a bit sorry for Amelia. A *bit*.

Tanya Harris and her partner, Alex Slater (one of the naughty boys I used to be scared of), do a brilliant presentation about how important bees are. And how they hope breeding programmes to save them will be as successful as the otter breeding programme has been. Tanya makes a few jokes about buzzing off, but overall she's actually a brilliant public speaker. I don't know why she was so against it at our comic launch all that time ago.

I know I'm probably biased but I think the ACE half of GUF do much better presentations than the CAC half of GUF.

Finally it is time for Nat and me to do our presentation. As we go up there and stand in front of our whole year, I feel like my knees are shaking,

but when I look down at them they aren't moving at all. Weird. And I have butterflies in my stomach as Natalie begins.

"We were particularly interested in birds and conservation, and that's why we wrote to Horace King," she says. (I think I see Amelia shake her head, laughing with Cassy in the crowd.) "And so of course we were particularly excited when he wrote back..." continues Natalie.

There is an audible gasp in the crowd at this. People are looking around at each other and then back at us, as if not quite sure if this is true. Amelia's mouth drops open.

Natalie continues her speech about how we met Poppy the famous owl. I hold up a big photograph of us with Horace and Poppy that my dad helped us blow up so people would be able to see it.

Then I take over the speaking and talk about how Horace told us all about conservation methods as he showed us round his sanctuary. I mention how it's important to protect creatures' natural habitats, like badgers'. (Natalie holds up my giant picture of a badger at this point.)

As I talk I grow in confidence, and though it's still

nerve-racking, I start to feel more normal and I get more comfortable in front of everyone. I feel pleased when we are finished.

Once everyone's been up, the judges have to go off and decide what they thought of the presentations and when they come back in, Mrs Unwin, the head of conservation planning, gives a quick speech about how impressed she is and how hard it was to judge because we've all done so well. Then they give out the prizes. Everyone gets a prize for something, but only *some* people get a Special Mention.

Joshua and Lewis win a prize for being the most inventive with the task. Megan and Emily win a prize for thinking about the practical application and benefits for everyone. Harriet wins a prize *and* a Special Mention for being so resourceful and informative. Amelia and Cassy win a prize for having such a beautifully put-together package, but they don't get a Special Mention. *a Special Mention...*

Finally it is announced that there is only one more Special Mention left to give. Cassy and Amelia nudge each other, looking relieved.

"Right then," says Mrs Unwin. "The last and final

Special Mention is awarded to Jessica and Natalie for artwork."

I don't *believe* it! Natalie nudges me and grins. We have to go up and receive our plastic medals while everyone claps. Well, nearly everyone. Amelia and Cassy aren't actually clapping. Joshua tries to do that whistle thing with his fingers and only partly succeeds.

Mrs Unwin puts the medals round our necks and shakes our hands. Then she addresses everyone and says, "This prize is because it is all very well *talking* about the environment and *writing* about the environment. But it is just as important to *show* what is great about the environment. In the future we will need a new generation of artists who will help keep the instinctive connection we feel with our wildlife alive. Pictures can conjure all kinds of feelings. Like the ones we judges all felt on seeing this beautiful badger."

I think I love the medal lady. She *gets* art! She likes pictures! She seems to know exactly what I was feeling when I drew the picture. I conveyed something in art! This is amazing!

Everyone is in high spirits afterwards as we are finally allowed to talk and start mixing and congratulating each other on our various successes. We get to have refreshments now – squash and biscuits for all our hard work. Today is a *good* day.

Joshua comes up to me. "Congrats on your picture," he says.

"Congrats on your presentation," I reply. "That was brilliant."

"Likewise your picture."

I see Amelia and Cassy across the room, talking crossly to each other. I can't believe they didn't clap when we won stuff. We clapped for *them*. It's like they want to be the only people that can be good at something. *Is that what I was like with Scarlett and the cartoons?* I wonder. I hope not.

I definitely need to stop worrying about the petty things, and live and let live. Actually, that gives me an idea for a cartoon…

I suddenly realise that Joshua is staring at me. "What?" I ask him.

"Nothing," he says. "I'm just glad we're friends again. I like it better when you're not storming out of things."

"Well, you're only human," I joke, *although if you think that's storming out, you haven't seen anything until you've met my Auntie Joan*, I think to myself. "Of course we're friends," I add.

"Good," he says. "Because I like you."

I laugh. He doesn't flinch, he just looks at me evenly. "Oh, right. You're serious," I say. "OK. Well, I like you too."

"Yeah! Group hug!" shouts Tanya Harris, grabbing both of us and shoving us together. "The old gang's back together!" She releases us. "I knew you'd change your mind, Toons."

"Will you rejoin the comic?" asks Joshua.

Hmmm. Well, I *did* say I wasn't going to be such an egotistical person and would get the other areas of my life in balance and everything. But I have *kind of*, pretty much *done* that now. And I have also just had an idea about a new cartoon…

"OK," I smile.

"Yeah!" Tanya pummels us into another hug.

WOOT!

"Woot woot," says Joshua, faintly sarcastically.

"I've been thinking," says Tanya, releasing us

again. "I think we need a website…"

And before I know it I am listening to Tanya's latest business plan. Maybe it will be fun. And anyway, I'm an *artist* now.

As I arrive home, for once I don't mind that the VanDerks are lurking by the hedge, waiting to pounce on my mum. But not because I can join in with the winning prizes contest, but because I feel like I have a *future*, and I don't care about them annoying me.

Everything is going to be brilliant. There's a lady with a proper job (who came to our school) who believes that art is *important* and that it speaks to people in indefinable and important ways.

But not only that, she believes in *my* art. My badger spoke to her. I might actually be good at something that people need in the *real world*. Not just cartoons (which they do need and are important, whatever anyone says) but drawing more serious stuff. I could try to draw more serious stuff. I will. Maybe I'll ask for some new pencils for my birthday.

"How did Jessica do today?" asks Mrs VanDerk. "Our Harriet got a *Special Mention*."

"Oh well, that's lovely," says my mum in her fake happy voice. "My little Jess got one too." She puts her arm around me. "I guess we're all in the prize gang together." She looks at them pointedly.

The VanDerks' smiles go tight and falter. I know they hate the idea of being in the same gang as my parents. But I still honestly think my mum is lowering herself to the VanDerks' level at the moment.

"Mum! Mum!" comes a shout from the street. We turn to see Auntie Joan and Tammy start down the garden path towards us with an excited cross-collie dog pulling hard on a leash.

"What the—" begins my mum.

"Hey, sweetie!" says Auntie Joan as the dog pulls at the lead and tries to bound towards my mum. "I got you this dog," she explains.

"She's rescued," says Tammy happily. There is a stony silence as my mum just stares at them in disbelief, and the dog nearly chokes itself trying to get free, and starts coughing.

"You're welcome," says my aunt cheerfully.

The VanDerks aren't even trying to hide their smirking at this point.

My Auntie Joan elaborates. "I said to Tammy, I

said, 'If you want anything done, you've got to go out and *make* it happen. Wishing won't make it so.' So I said to her, 'You want to rescue that dog? You just rescue that dog.' I get things done. 'Just do it.' That's what I say."

So this is what happens if people actually live their lives by the Nike advertising slogan, I think. They get Kit Kats and dogs.

My mum finally finds her voice. "Oh *God*, get in the house," she hisses, glancing at the VanDerks.

"Cheerio!" wave the VanDerks gleefully.

"Can we keep him?" I blurt out, following them into the front door.

"Inside," hisses my mum, "Cheery bye!" she simpers to the VanDerks.

The door slams. There is quite a row.

But I don't care, because I am an *artist* as well as a cartoonist; Natalie is my best friend forever; I am a sane member of an ace comic; and now we even have a dog.